THE CREPE MAKERS'
BOND

Julie Crabtree

milkweed
editions

© 2011, Text by Julie Crabtree
All rights reserved. Except for brief quotations in critical articles or reviews, no part of this book may be reproduced in any manner without prior written permission from the publisher: Milkweed Editions, 1011 Washington Avenue South, Suite 300, Minneapolis, Minnesota 55415.
(800) 520-6455
www.milkweed.org

Published 2011 by Milkweed Editions
Printed in Canada by Friesens Corporation
Cover design by Kristine Mudd
Cover photo © Ocean/Corbis
Interior design by Ann Sudmeier
The text of this book is set in Warnock Pro by BookMobile Design
    and Publishing Services
11 12 13 14 15   5 4 3 2 1
First Edition

Manufactured in Manitoba in 2011 by Friesens Corporation.

Please turn to the back of this book for a list of the sustaining funders of Milkweed Editions.

Library of Congress Cataloging-in-Publication Data

Crabtree, Julie.
    The crepe makers' bond / Julie Crabtree. — 1st ed.
        p.   cm.
    Summary: Fourteen-year-old Ariel uses cooking to work through problems, but none of her recipes are likely to help when she and Nicki learn that M may be moving away from Alameda soon after they begin eighth grade. Includes recipes and cooking tips.
    ISBN 978-1-57131-695-0 (pbk. : alk. paper) — ISBN 978-1-57131-693-6 (hardcover : alk. paper)
    [1. Best friends—Fiction. 2. Friendship—Fiction. 3. Cooking—Fiction. 4. Family life—California—Fiction. 5. Middle schools—Fiction. 6. Schools —Fiction. 7. Moving, Household—Fiction. 8. Alameda (Calif—Fiction.] I. Title.
    PZ7.C84152Cre 2010
    [Fic]—dc22

                                                                    2010020141

This book is printed on acid-free paper.

For Jay

The Crepe Makers' Bond

The Taste of Poetry

Food is the poetry
of the mouth,
in its combinations comes
the exquisite tastes of life.

In delicate preparations,
the master chef
pours his heart out,
an exquisite art form.

Time honored tradition,
dedicated for human pleasure,
delivering music in its consumption,
arousing sense of taste.

In a mixture of spices,
the sweet blending,
simmering treasure of innovation,
sparkling liquor of interaction,
the notes come together
in a meal of perfection.

—David Lester Young
June 21, 2003

A note from Ariel

You are about to read the story of one crazy year in my life. When I remember all that happened, both the great and the really sad, it's mixed together with all the things I made in the kitchen. That might seem weird, but I find making fantastic food gives me sanity. I can't tell you this story without also telling you about what was going on in my kitchen as everything unfolded. These recipes are mixed in with the chapters, and there's also a listing of them in the back of the book. They are my own, and I hope you'll try them for yourself. I have also included some of the tips and tricks I have learned over the years as I've studied the art of food. Maybe you too will make something really fabulous despite the drama all around you.

THE CREPE MAKERS'
BOND

Prologue
Earthquake

The earthquake started like they always do. Suddenly.
Nicki and M were sitting on barstools watching me
fold wontons one minute; the next second we were all
thrown on the floor. I instinctively crouched against
the cabinets as the wavelike motion of the earth
rattled the flour canister off the counter. It hit my arm
on its way down. My hearing became incredibly sharp
and I instantly registered clacking silverware, pots and
pans jingling deep within the cabinets, glasses and
bowls clattering delicately, and the jarring blare of
dozens of car alarms outside. My own sharp breath-
ing was loudest of all. The floor's vibration traveled
through my knees and hummed in my belly. Shredded
carrots and a wonton wrapper tumbled from the
counter and landed next to me.

M yelled, "Stay down, Nicki!"

I heard Nicki say something but the fruit bowl clattered to the ground just then and I couldn't make out her words, only the fear. An apple rolled to a stop against my leg and, insanely, I wondered if the fall had bruised it.

Then, just as suddenly, it stopped. I stood up cautiously and peeked out the window. A hose reel had tumbled onto my mother's border of violets, smashing their delicate purple heads into the dirt. Our neighbor's wind chime had fallen and shattered.

Nicki's voice startled me out of my trance. "Are you both okay?"

I looked over at M, who was picking up paper napkins that had dropped to the floor with the first jolt. She nodded. No one said anything else. It was one of those weird frozen-in-time moments, like we were just hovering in space. I realized it was the absolute motionlessness of the earth that created this sensation.

There is no more complete feeling of stillness than right after an earthquake. You can't imagine how stable ground feels like such a gift. You want to trust it, but you can't. There are always aftershocks, little jolts and pulses beneath your feet reminding you that nothing is ever completely reliable. Not even the ground under your feet.

In my mind I always see that day, the day of the quake, as the point when things began to shift between me and M and Nicki. I began to see everything that happened as either before the quake or after the quake. It marked the start of the hardest year of my life. Well, my life so far.

It's funny that the quake became such a turning point for me because it was only a medium strength earthquake. No one in Alameda or anywhere else was killed. The broken stuff got swept up and thrown away, the cabinets got straightened, and everyone's stories of where they were and what they were doing when it hit were told and then forgotten. But I still think of the quake as something that started a chain reaction somehow. Like the universe was trying to tell me something about the next few months.

I know none of this makes sense now. Maybe it will later on.

Shaky Ground Stuffed Wontons with Peanut Sauce

1 package small, square wonton wrappers (in the produce
    section usually, refrigerated)

½ C. peanut oil

1 small bag shredded carrots

2 boneless, skinless chicken breasts, cooked and chopped
    (pre-cooked or even deli chicken works if you're in a
    hurry)

¼ C. honey-roasted peanuts, chopped

½ C. bottled peanut sauce (in the Asian food section)

*Toss carrots, chicken, peanuts and ¼ C. peanut sauce in a
bowl. Stuff the wontons by putting a heaping tablespoon of
filling in the middle of each square, then folding it over so the
ends come together to form a triangle. Use wet fingers (have a
bowl with water near to dip your fingers in) to seal the edges
together. You can also use a fork to make little crimps around
the edges, which looks pretty but is more time-consuming.
Heat oil in a skillet until very hot (flick a drop of water in it,
and if it immediately sizzles, it's hot enough). Cook wontons
about a minute on each side, until golden brown. Drain on
paper towels. Can serve hot or at room temperature. Arrange
on a tray with a little bowl of remaining peanut sauce for
dipping.*

First Day of School

My obnoxiously loud alarm works its way into my brain. It takes me a minute to wake up enough to realize it isn't part of my dream. I hit the snooze button to buy eight more precious minutes before I have to force myself out of bed.

I stayed up way too late last night. Every article of clothing I own is either on my floor (rejected) or draped over my desk chair (possibly to be worn for the first day of eighth grade). The goal is to look great while also looking like I didn't try hard to look great. My outfit can't come across as too . . . effortful. It might be impossible.

And I have the whole chest issue to deal with. M and Nicki say I'm lucky, but they have no idea how hard it is to be this "developed." Anything low-cut or slightly tight makes me look like I am trying to show off, which I am not. I hate the stares actually. Anything baggy makes me look shapeless and fat, which I am not either. Sigh.

Having red hair on top of the aforementioned "blessing" makes it just plain hard to blend in. And I am only five feet tall, which is a whole other area of difficulty. Despite my many issues, I want my first-day outfit to give me a chance to make a new impression. I know most of the kids already, but every first day feels like a new start. Hopeful. I was thinking about this last night as I tried on and discarded T-shirts, sundresses, capris, and jeans. Nothing seemed right. What I really needed was a box of hair color, a new minimizer bra, and a sudden growth spurt.

Last night I'd called M, hoping we could whine together about having nothing to wear, but she already had her outfit ready to go: low-rise camo pants from Old Navy, narrow black belt with small silver studs, and a black, long-sleeved T-shirt under her white, short-sleeved T-shirt from Banana Republic. Her aunt had given her a shark's tooth necklace from Hawaii, threaded on a rough-cut leather string, and it will perfectly complete her outfit. She'll look cool and causal and a tiny bit edgy, but not like she *tried* hard. She had nailed it and I was jealous.

Lucky M, she sounded happy to go back to school. I wondered briefly if this was the same best friend who just last year kept a "Days to Parole" flip calendar counting down the days of school left.

I called Nicki next, thinking (okay, hoping) she might be having the same struggles on this first-day eve. Nicki has that kind of lithe, proportioned body that looks good in everything, plus an exotic, pretty face. She's part American Indian. We have been teased at school for being "princesses." It *is* undeniable that Nicki really does look like the Disney Pocahontas.

But me . . . I got named for the ridiculously perky mermaid Ariel because I was born with red hair. Cute, right? Not so much. They might as well have tattooed Disney's logo on my forehead. At least Pocahontas is a real historical figure who was brave and smart. Ariel is a ditsy cartoon mermaid who wears a shell bra and combs her hair with a fork. M, the lucky girl, doesn't have a princess label.

Honestly, Nicki is gorgeous and elegant enough to be a *real* princess. I would probably hate her except that she is totally clueless about how pretty she is. And Nicki is just, well, nice. Oh, and for the record, I think I am a nice person too, and I am nowhere near as air-headed as *that* Ariel. Anyway, I am getting off the subject. Bringing up the princess thing is bound to set me off on one of my "issues."

Back to last night. Nicki was also trying on clothes when I called after dinner, but had narrowed down her choices. She is modest, so her choices—long, granny-style gauzy dress she got at the flea market, or her GLO jeans with an empire-waisted loose tunic—were typical. She'll look great in either. Plus, Nicki is the yearbook girl at school, and she'll be so focused on getting her pictures that she won't even worry about how she looks. The girl lives and breathes yearbook. It is her obsession, like cooking is mine.

Anyway, she tried to tell me how good I look in a couple of outfits I was considering, but Nicki is so loyal and kind she is not to be relied on for hard truths. Like *Your chest looks enormous in that.* Like *There's nothing that makes someone who's barely five feet look tall.*

I was more depressed than ever after I got off the phone with Nicki. It was almost ten o'clock by then. I couldn't try on any more clothes, and I was too keyed-up to sleep. I needed to calm down and chill out, so I headed to the kitchen. It is my salvation.

When I'm whisking a sauce or kneading dough or chopping onions I feel calm and capable, like I can handle anything. I needed to put my first-day outfit and consequent nerves into perspective. So even though it was late, I decided to make a special something to take to school tomorrow for Nicki and M. They are my faithful tasters, and I love trying out new recipes on them. When I am a professional chef I will name one of my dishes after them, or maybe I'll dedicate a cookbook to them.

As always, I lost track of time as I worked. I used the mandolin slicer to cut two English cucumbers into rounds so thin they were transparent. I salted them heavily and sandwiched them between a bunch of paper towels, then plopped a cutting board on top to squeeze out the water. At that point my dad came in and lectured me about going to bed, but I knew he wouldn't do anything if I stayed up late. My dad tries hard, but he really can't discipline.

As I toasted sesame seeds I thought again about yesterday's earthquake, and about this legend Nicki told us. It was a story her grandma used to tell about earthquakes. The story is basically that the Earth is a living creature that has the same kinds of problems people have. Sometimes it gets sick with fever and chills, which we experience as earthquakes. As I watched the little seeds pop and singe in the frying pan, I thought about how we would help the earth get better. Were you supposed to starve a fever or feed it? I can never remember.

It was midnight by the time I finished making the sesame cucumbers. We were out of seasoned rice vinegar, so I ended up spending a long time making a vinegar bath from scratch. The first batch had too much sherry, and in the second I overdid the sesame oil and it tasted heavy. I finally got it just right. I layered the delicate cucumber rounds in my Tupperware cake carrier (it's great for lots of things besides just cake), sprinkled on the sesame seeds, and snipped a few fresh chives over them for garnish before jamming the container in the fridge.

I will admit that I fussed a lot with this fairly simple dish, but I had to work until I got that good, bone-tired sensation that means I'll sleep heavily and dreamlessly. I always get it if I work in the kitchen long enough. I guess I was pretty anxious about school starting.

So now it's morning. I didn't get enough sleep and I feel cranky. My hair smells like vinegar from last night. I don't have time to wash it. I can't hit snooze again, and I have to commit to some outfit in the next half hour. I have a feeling of dread. Oh well, at least I have M and Nicki. And a cake carrier full of sesame cucumbers . . . what more could a girl need on her first day of eighth grade?

Too Cool for School
Cucumber Salad

2 English cucumbers (long, shrink-wrapped cucumbers,
    sometimes called hot house cucumbers—regular
    cucumbers can be used, but they aren't as good and
    they must be peeled)

3 T. salt

seasoned rice vinegar

1 t. sesame oil

white pepper

2 T. sesame seeds

2 T. snipped chives (or substitute green onions or
    spring onions)

Slice cucumbers into thin slices. (A mandolin slicer is best for getting thin, even slices, but be sure to use the hand guard— the blade is very sharp on this type of slicer. Check out the scar on my left thumb for proof.) Gently toss cucumbers with salt, coating both sides. Lay several layers of paper towel on a flat surface and arrange cucumbers on toweling so they are flat and not overlapping. Lay several more layers of towels over them, and place a cutting board or large book on top. Let cucumbers be pressed for at least 20 minutes, preferably an hour. While they are getting the water squished out of them, toast the sesame seeds in a small pan over medium heat. When they are golden and fragrant, remove them to a small bowl (if you leave them in the hot pan they'll keep cooking and burn). Put cucumber slices in a bowl and gently toss them with the vinegar, sesame oil, and pepper. Let them marinate in bowl, covered, overnight, or at least a few hours. To serve, take them out of the vinegar bath, put them on a large platter and sprinkle with the sesame seeds and chives.

First Day Catastrophe

We had agreed to meet at M's house because it is clos-
est to school, and her mom will drop us off. Our middle school is within walking distance, but we always
run late in the morning. Besides, M's mom doesn't
mind driving us as long as she doesn't have to get out
of the car. It's part of her therapy for having issues
about going out of the house.

It is so foggy this morning that San Francisco is
completely invisible. Alameda feels lonely when it's like
this, as though it is cut off from the world. Isolated.
Technically Alameda is an island, but barely; you
could easily throw a rock across to Oakland from the
shore. When it gets foggy though, it feels like we could
be floating in some remote ocean. It makes me want
to live somewhere else, somewhere more connected,
when it's like this.

The "cone zone" is filled with a long line of cars. M's mom pulls into the line and we inch forward, watching as several kids hop out of the minivan ahead of us. These kids are fresh from elementary school. They look scared and hopeful. One of the girls frantically checks her face in the car's side mirror and jerks back from her mother's attempt to kiss her cheek. We say nothing, but I know we are all remembering our first day. It seems like decades ago, not just last year. We are so different now.

Finally, we pull into the getting-out part of the cone zone. We grab our backpacks and pile out of the car. M's mom blows us each little air kisses. We each jump or lunge to catch the invisible kisses and smack our empty palms on our cheeks. It's one of those things we have done with each other's moms forever. Here we go, another year begins.

"Ariel, that black shirt is *perfect*," Nicki pats my arm, "I don't know why you were stressing so much last night. With your shape, you always look good." This is *so* Nicki. Lies with good intentions. I snort and give her a little shove.

"What'd you make, Ariel?" M points to the cake carrier I'm carrying. M and Nicki know they are in for something at lunch when they see the carrier.

"Just a light cucumber salad. A side dish. I felt like making something last night, and we had a bunch of English cucumbers . . ." I trail off. They've had the salad before, though not with the homemade vinegar. I think they'll notice the improvement.

"Yum. I love that!" Nicki claps.

"Oh, isn't that the one with the gross red onions?" M asks. Geez, where's the gratitude?

"M, I snipped *chives* on them this time, so quit whining." I roll my eyes and M giggles. I know all their picky food issues pretty well by now, and I knew M wouldn't eat the salad with red onion.

"Thank GOD." She breathes out as though she had been holding her breath. M is so funny with her fake dramatics. She stopped doing it, stopped being herself, for awhile last year. It's nice to see her funny and happy again.

Last year was really crazy for her. It is all too long and complicated to go into here, but if you want to read about everything that happened to M, she has a book that tells the whole story. I'll just say that now, while her mom is still somewhat whacked out and her dad is still basically absent, I think M is alright.

And Nicki? Honestly, I don't know for sure about her. Last year M was kind of the center of our attention, so maybe I didn't take in Nicki's issues so much. Lately, I have started noticing some weird things with Nicki. She is kind of . . . distracted. I get the feeling she is guarding something, but I have no idea what. Maybe the earthquake jarred loose my paranoid chip.

On the first day of school the whole place, teachers

and kids, janitors and overly involved parents, gather on the basketball court. The principal gives a speech, we say the pledge of allegiance, and general announcements are made. As everyone gathers, the various cliques group together, talking excitedly, glancing around to see the other clumps of kids. The new kids and loners form a raggedy fringe around the edges, hoping to be included in any of the established groups. Good luck. This first day dictates more or less who will hang with whom for the year. Everyone notices everyone else.

We three are, of course, standing in our own little cluster. There's a group of jocks behind us, and I hear the low murmur-chuckle-snort sounds that mean they are talking about my chest. I learned long ago to both recognize and ignore it.

Our principal steps under the basketball hoop with a microphone. She is the tiniest adult I have ever seen (she's even a tad shorter than me, which is seriously shrimpy), but she is tough as nails. She taps the cord-less mike and the huge speakers set up against the bleachers whine deafening feedback. Everyone groans and hands clap over ears. If any dogs were in the area they probably keeled over.

We all turn toward her, ready to hear the predict-able speech about what a fantastic year this will be because the teachers are so incredible and the students are so wonderful and all that. Then she says, "Ariel Solomon, please go the office immediately."

The whole student body looks in my direction. Even the kids who don't know me. I feel my face flame and I know it matches my hair. I want to sink through the concrete. I try to look unconcerned as I turn toward the office, but I trip on the cucumber salad I had put down near my feet. The boys behind us laugh, and I hear titters from other groups. Forget sinking through the floor, how about a swift and painless death? M pats my back and Nicki whispers something meant to comfort me. I walk quickly toward the office wondering why I have to go there, and why the universe sees fit, in literally the first minutes of a new school year, to humiliate me. It's unbelievable.

My mom is standing at the counter chatting with Ms. Patel, the school secretary, as I enter the office.

"Mom?"

She turns toward me and smiles. In her hand she holds my compact bee sting kit. Cheerfully, she thrusts the bright yellow box toward me. "You forgot this, and you know you should have it here at school."

She sees from my look that I am less than thrilled.

"You called me out of the assembly, *on the PA system*, to give me a bee sting kit? Mom, they have one in the nurse's office! And what are the chances I would get stung today? I haven't even *seen* a bee around here in like a year."

She looks confused, maybe a little hurt. "Ariel, I was only trying to help. You know how allergic you are—remember last time? You could end up in the hospital . . ."

I snatch the kit, interrupting, "Thanks, Mom." I try to keep the sarcasm out, but it is hopeless. My words are sharp and angry. The secretary is suddenly very busy with some papers behind her desk.

My mom sighs and gives me that injured-mother look I can't stand. I feel instantly guilty. She waves to Ms. Patel, and brushes past me out the door, muttering something about ingratitude and anaphylactic shock. I stare after her, the plastic box handle cutting into my fingers as I grip it. The secretary tries to act like she hasn't been listening to everything as she picks up a small tube and squeezes sludgy, overly sweet hand lotion onto her palm. A drop glops onto her desk. It looks like melted brie cheese, which makes me feel even worse because baked brie is my mom's favorite appetizer on the planet. I'll make it tonight, I think, as an apology.

I shake my head and refocus—I still have a day to get through. It is 8:38 in the morning of the first day of eighth grade and I have already managed to embarrass myself in front of the whole school *and* hurt my mom's feelings. If I believed in signs, I would be very, very concerned about what this means for my immediate future.

Guilty Daughter
Baked Brie

1 tube crescent rolls
cooking spray
1 round of brie cheese, rind (that's the hard outer part)
    removed
¼ C. chopped green olives
¼ C. chopped black olives
1 T. chopped, fresh parsley or 1 t. dried

Preheat oven to 350°. Pop and unroll dough into one big
rectangle. If it breaks apart at the seams, mash it back
together with your fingers. Spray a cookie sheet with nonstick
spray, and lay the rectangle of dough on it. Put cheese in
the middle and sprinkle the olives and parsley on top of the
cheese. Fold the dough over the cheese, carefully pinching
the ends together to completely enclose the cheese. Make it
look like a wrapped Hershey's Kiss shape-wise. Use kitchen
scissors or a sharp knife to trim it into an even shape where it
"gathers." Bake for about 20 minutes, until the dough is lightly
browned. Let it cool for 10 minutes. Serve with crackers or
breadsticks.

A Major Misunderstanding

I join my homeroom, already in progress, and take a vacant seat near the back. Nicki and M are in a different homeroom this year, so I am on my own. Mr. Kraft, a science teacher who knows me already, just raises an eyebrow in my direction and keeps talking. He even gives me a little half smile, which doesn't make any sense. He is the type that will say something sarcastic about students coming in late, but he surprises me with silence on my tardiness. I am grateful but confused. He is talking about his strict attendance and tardy policy, so I can zone out. I've heard it before.

The morning passes quickly. It seems like last year, more or less. A few new faces drift by in the halls, the classes are different, but it all feels the same. I am on guard for people making fun of me for the PA announcement and for tripping like I did, but strangely no one says anything. In fact, several kids actually give me what appear to be looks of sympathy. Kayla, the undisputed leader of the most elite, popular girl pack at school, even says hi and pats my shoulder. I don't think she's even noticed I exist before. Wow, could it be possible that the normal savagery of junior high has been replaced with kindness and sympathy? I can't wait to talk to Nicki and M about all this.

At lunch we meet up at our usual table next to the temporary building. M sits with her elbows propped on the cake carrier full of cucumber salad, which I left when I stumbled my way to the office this morning. Her face is tilted toward the bright sun, which just broke through the fog minutes ago. Her eyes are squinched and she doesn't see me approach. Nicki's not here yet.

"Hola Ms. Mattie-M-Matilda," I call out as I approach. When she was going through all her name confusion I made up this name, which encompasses all the different phases of name she's been through. She says it sounds like a crazy old lady from a children's book, but it makes her smile.

She isn't smiling now though. Her eyes snap fully open and she looks at me with a little furrow of worry running across her forehead. "I can't even believe you are still *here*," she says.

I think she's being overly dramatic. Yes, I was totally humiliated this morning, but everyone's been so nice. I'm really not even feeling upset about it anymore.

"Actually, I'm over it, M." I grab the Tupperware and take off the lid. "In fact, I think everyone's grown up a lot around here. I mean, no one's been anything but cool. Even *Kayla* was sweet to me . . ."

I stop talking because Nicki has raced up. She is stuffing her "emergency only" cell phone into her pocket. She sits at the table, eyeing me very intensely.

"You okay?" She's staring at me as though I am fragile.

"What is it with you guys? I mean, I got paged and then tripped in front of the school. It wasn't a *stellar* experience, but I didn't pee my pants or barf or something!"

As I talk I smooth the cucumber slices into little fans and slide them to the middle of the table. M takes two and crunches slowly, still staring at me as though I might break down at any moment.

Nicki is straddling the bench so she is staring at my profile. Her body posture says she is ready to hug me or hold me up at any second. I turn my head toward her and give her my best one-raised-eyebrow look.

"I guess being here is probably easiest anyway," she says, in what I know is her soothing voice. She uses it when her baby brother is crying. My humiliation is hitting them harder than me. Weird.

Nicki puts her hand on my arm. "Air, I have never even told you about going through stuff like this. I mean about . . . *loss* . . . or just even almost losing someone. . . . I know this is hard . . ." Nicki is stringing out her words, pausing a lot. I am not one to curse, but what the hell? What is she talking about? Does Nicki have some secret story? I *knew* something odd was going on with her! But why is she rubbing my arm as if I am going to break down at any moment? Will Rod Serling be making an appearance soon?

I shake my head and shrug. "Nick, what are you talking about?"

Nicki seems to snap out of some trance and she jerks back her arm, shakes her head a little and says, with a forced smile, "Oh, nothing, never mind, you don't have to talk about it. I just hope you're okay." She sounds fakely cheerful.

"I am *fine.* Over it." They both just stare back. Awkward silence. Last week's earthquake pops into my mind. I think it knocked a few screws loose in my friends' heads.

A change of subject is in order. "Did I tell you guys I'm going to enter the Idaho potato baking contest? I have made my twice-baked recipe five times now, and it is supremely yummy. . . ." I trail off because they are both looking confused. "Um, is there something sinister about potatoes? You guys are acting freaky."

There is an expectant silence as though they are waiting for more from me. I feel out of sync with them—kinda like the feeling you get when the soundtrack doesn't match the picture on a TV show and the person's mouth moves a second after you hear their words.

"Maybe talking about her cooking is helping her cope," Nicki says to M.

I am going to slap these two in a minute. Why can't they let it go?

"Is he going to make it?" M asks in a voice barely above a whisper.

"Who?" We are officially in the Twilight Zone. What is she talking about?

"Your dad," they both stage-whisper at once, and neither says "jinx."

There're a few seconds of silence as I try to make sense of this. We were talking potatoes, weren't we? Where on the planet does my dad fit in here?

"My dad?" I finally ask, still not comprehending.

Now *they* look confused. M cocks her head at me and squints her eyes. "Everyone heard. It was on the police scanner the janitor keeps in the side office. It was your dad they said. He had a heart attack or stroke or something. He collapsed, a bunch of people saw it! That's why you got called to the office this morning. That's why your mom was here." Nicki is nodding, agreeing with M.

"What . . . *what*? WHAT?" It's the only word I can muster.

Nicki makes a little cucumber stack in the container, waiting for me to say something else, but I can't.

I feel like someone dropped me on an alien planet and forgot to tell me what language the natives speak.

"Maybe it wasn't a heart attack?" M finally asks.

Suddenly I flash on a bunch of little moments from my morning: the looks of sympathy and kind glances from normally mean or indifferent kids, Mr. Kraft tactfully ignoring my late entry into homeroom, the click of Kayla's French manicure as she brushed my shoulder. They thought something had happened to my dad. It suddenly makes sense. But it also makes no sense. How did we go from a bee sting kit to this? If something did happen to him, my mom would have told me when she was here, right?

"It was my bee allergy stuff," I say dumbly to Nicki and M.

Now they look lost. I start to explain, but only get to the part about going to the school office and seeing my mom there. I stop talking when Jerrod, a really cute guy from the water polo team, passes by and says, "Hang in there, Ariel."

And just like that I choose to play a part. "Thanks, Jerrod, I will," I say and smile bravely. Jerrod winks and gives me a thumbs-up.

M and Nicki just stare at me.

For once all three of us are speechless.

Once Misunderstood
Twice Baked Potatoes

4 large baking potatoes
2 T. butter
¼ C. or less milk
½ C. sharp cheddar cheese, grated
5 slices bacon, cooked crisp and crumbled
1 T. grated onion
1 t. minced garlic
salt and pepper
crushed (seasoned) dry stuffing mix

Preheat oven to 425°. Scrub potatoes and prick several times with a fork (or they will explode and dump potato guts all over your oven—trust me on this). Put potatoes directly on middle rack in oven and bake about 35 minutes, or until they feel soft and squishy inside when poked. Using a kitchen towel or pot holder, remove them and cut them in half. Use a spoon to scoop the soft baked potato into a bowl. Use an electric mixer to beat the potatoes with the milk. Use just enough milk to make the potatoes creamy but still very thick. Stir in all the other ingredients. Spoon the potato mixture back into the skins. Put them in a 13x9" pan, cover with tin foil, and return to oven for 15 minutes.

My Really Old, Kinda Famous Dad

I should back up and explain something about my dad
and why it is in the realm of the believable that he had
a stroke or something. And why everyone would care
if he did. The first thing is he's old. Really old. Sixty-six
"years young," as he likes to say (and I hate that stupid
expression more than you can ever know). He is my
mom's second husband.

Mom married hubby numero uno right out of college, and they got divorced when she was twenty-eight.
They lived in San Francisco and didn't have kids. They
drank a lot of coffee at little artsy cafés and took ball-
room dancing lessons. They were like *that*. I met "Stan
the Ex" one time when we went to Disney World in
Florida. He lives in Florida now. We met up with him
at a dingy IHOP and my mom and he quizzed each
other about old friends and acted quite friendly over a

stack of buttermilk pancakes, while Ryan and I shredded napkins and kicked each other under the table in
boredom.

Stan seemed nice actually. Apparently, and these
are my mother's words, they "were more like pals with
mutual friends and shared activities, but not much
else, so we decided to move on and stay friendly." I
always thought the idea of a nice divorce was odd. I
mean, you're purposefully killing this really serious
relationship, and that can be friendly? M and I have
talked about this a lot because her parents also had a
friendly divorce. But that's different.

I remember watching Stan closely, imagining him
as my father. Obviously, if he was I wouldn't be *me*, I
mean the genes and all, but I wondered what it would
be like if Mom had decided to have kids with him. I
guess I wouldn't be here at all, but in a purely imagina-
tive way, I could see having a dad like Stan . . . so *young*
and cute and normal. It made me ashamed thinking
like that, like I was betraying my own father, which I
guess I was. My dad is old, no way around that. It has
embarrassed me a lot over the years. Strangers sometimes think he's my grandfather.

My mom divorced Stan and thought she'd be a
single gal forever, but then my dad came along. Mom
was working at McPherson and Kidd, this huge law
firm in San Francisco, and Dad came in one day to
sign some stuff. He was a client, there for his business

(more on that later), and Mom brought him Earl Grey tea and papers to sign. Dad complimented Mom's silver bracelet. Mom noticed Dad's thick white hair and thought it was distinguished (me and Ryan always groan at this part of the story). Dad was in his late forties, and Mom was like thirty.

My parents will launch into this "how we met" story at the slightest mention of the subject. It is creepy but cute at the same time. They got married six months after their first encounter. My brother Ryan was born eleven months after that, and I was born a couple of years after Ryan. By then my dad was fifty-three.

Everyone knows him too. My dad has lived in Alameda his whole life. His family has run a candy and confection store called Island Sweets since 1922. My dad took it over from Grandpa when he was still in his twenties, and has personally made it the loud, popular, crowded place it is today. Every kid in Alameda has eaten a Chocolate Lava Lover's Birthday Cakelet (you get one for free on your birthday). Dad also does these zany ads on local cable where he acts like different characters from movies and does little spoofy skits that somehow involve stuff the store sells. All of them are quite embarrassing. He has tried to get Ryan and me to be in a couple, but there is a less than zero chance I would ever do it. The ads are seriously dorky.

All this is to say that my dad is old and well-known here in Alameda. His name on a police scanner is something people would notice and want to gossip about. It is a freakish coincidence that my mom came to school *and* this rumor about Dad happened at the same time. I need to call home and ask my mom about this crazy story, and then figure out how to handle the other kids.

Dang though, it is really cool having everyone pay so much attention to me (and not because of my bra size or my hair color) and be so nice. I wish, in a weird way, it were true about Dad. I mean, true that something dramatic happened to him, but that he is okay and all, of course. Then I could keep the sympathy wagon rolling. I think I might be a bad person for just admitting that.

Nicki and M can help me get sorted, so I turn to them and begin to talk.

Chocolate Lava Lover's
Happy Birthday Cakelet

For the "lava" center

1 large bar dark chocolate
½ C. evaporated milk (NOT sweetened condensed milk,
    that kind is totally different)

For the cakelets

8 oz. semisweet chocolate chips
2 sticks unsalted butter
4 eggs
1 C. white sugar
2 t. vanilla
⅔ C. flour (sifted if it's lumpy)
cooking spray

Melt the chocolate bar in a bowl in the microwave for about one minute, or until it is melted enough to stir smooth. Mix in the evaporated milk with a fork until it's totally mixed into the chocolate. Put the bowl in the refrigerator. Preheat oven to 375°. Use either 6 giant-size muffin tins or 12 regular-size muffin tins, and coat them with cooking spray. Melt chocolate chips in a bowl in the oven as it preheats, or in the microwave until totally melted (about 1 minute). Melt the butter and mix it into the melted chocolate chips. Set aside. Mix eggs, sugar, and vanilla with an electric mixer for about 5 minutes, or until the mixture is very smooth and creamy looking. Add the chocolate/butter mixture and mix it in well. Add the flour and mix it only long enough for the flour to disappear, no longer, or the cake will be tough. Divide the cake batter into equal portions in the muffin tins. Get the chocolate "lava" bowl from the refrigerator. Using your hands, roll the mixture into the same number of chocolate balls as muffin tins filled with batter. Put a chocolate ball in the middle of the batter in each one. Bake about 20 minutes, or until the cake springs back when lightly poked. Cool in the tins for 10 minutes, then run a knife around edges and carefully remove them by turning the tins upside down on a counter or cutting board. Serve warm with a scoop of vanilla ice cream.

It's a Mafia Thing

Nicki has a cell phone, but she is only allowed to use
it for emergencies. Over the summer, on at least two
occasions, M and I have seen Nicki pretend to be
doing something, like going to the bathroom, when
she is actually using the "emergency" phone. I asked
her straight-out once who she was calling, and she
snapped and said she was checking on her brother. But
why would she sneak away to call her parents about
her brother? I'd started to push her on it, but the look
in her eyes stopped me. Nicki seems shy and gentle,
but she can get crazy angry. It flashes in her eyes and
you just know not to cross her. It only happens once in
awhile, but lately it usually involves her phone.

This is why I am cautious about asking her to use
it now. I form prayer hands and ask Nicki, "Can I use
your phone to call my mom really quick? I need to

figure out this mess, and you know M and I don't have cell phones."

Nicki shakes her head. "Sorry, Air, but this isn't really an emergency . . ."

M interrupts her, "God, Nicki, it might be. We don't know if maybe something *did* happen to Mr. Solomon."

Nicki shrugs, looking a little apologetic, and says, "Obviously it is just a weird misunderstanding. I would let you call, Ariel, but my parents monitor the minutes. You know how strict they are, they would take it away if they thought I was letting my friends use it."

I drop my hands and sigh. That phone will only see action if something is on fire or someone is bleeding. She is *so* responsible, I swear. Then again, it seems like she must have quite a few "emergencies" lately, the way we have seen her talking hurriedly between classes and by the bathroom during study hall.

There is no point arguing with her anymore. She is not going to bend. We decide I will have to ask to use the office phone.

I give Nicki a look and get up. "I guess you guys will have to get to your next class, so see ya."

"Don't be mad, Ariel." Nicki is looking down as she speaks, twirling her hair.

"We could go with you," M cuts in. "I don't care if we get detention . . ." The shrill of the five minute bell cuts her off.

"Thanks, M, but it's okay, I'll see you guys after class." I pat her arm and trudge across the blacktop toward the office. I can hear the soft rise and fall of Nicki and M talking as I walk away.

Mom picks up on the second ring. "Hi!" she says, all cheerful. Caller ID, she must think it's Ms. Patel.

"Mom, it's me."

"Oh, yes, Ariel." She's still upset with me—her voice assumes the injured, slightly cold tone she gets when she's sulking.

"Mom, is everything okay with Dad?"

"Your father? Well, yes, of course, Ariel. He's filming the *Godfather* commercial. You know, we talked about it last night."

I am possibly the only fourteen-year-old girl on the continent who has actually seen *The Godfather* several times. It is the classic of classics for mafia movies, which I adore. In fact, I am the one who gave Dad the idea to spoof it for his next commercial.

"But he's okay and everything?"

"Ariel, what is this about?" Mom asks me sharply. "If you called to apologize for your rude behavior this morning, just say so. You don't need to act like you were calling for some other reason and then . . ."

I cut her off impatiently, "Someone heard that Dad had a heart attack. On the police scanner here? I was confused, because you were just here to give me the bee kit and why wouldn't you tell me if Dad got sick?"

39

Mom is quiet.

"Mom?"

"I . . . I . . . don't know anything about this, Ariel."
Her voice sounds scared.

"You mean it might be true?" I feel tears spring to
my eyes and I realize I am holding the phone in a death
grip.

Mom sucks in her breath like she always does when
she is upset but taking charge. Her voice still has a
quaver in it as she says, "Honey, I will get to the bottom
of this. You sit tight, stay in the office, and I'll call back
as soon as I know what's going on."

"Okay, but . . ." I am about to ask her to come get
me—I don't want to sit here waiting—but she has already hung up. I hand the phone back to Ms. Patel.

"Everything okay, hon?" she asks me.

"My mom is going to call back," I tell her. "I need to
wait here."

"Wait in the nurse's office if you want," Ms. Patel
gestures toward the closet-sized office behind the
counter.

"Okay, thanks." I am grateful to be somewhere
that's not so public. I am still trying to keep from
crying. I lay down on the padded table, the crunchy
paper covering scrunches up under my shoulders in
an uncomfortable lump. I close my eyes. I can't stand
waiting. I try not to think. Isn't that what meditation
is? I can't do it. I am thinking about what not to think

about. I sit up and start ripping the crunchy paper into little flakes. I put them in my pocket.

Ms. Patel sticks her head around the corner. "Ariel, it's your mother. You can take it in here." She picks up a wall-mounted phone, pushes a blinking light and hands me the receiver. Then she just stands there.

I press the receiver into my chest and give her a tight smile. I am not going to hear potentially terrible news with her standing over me. "Thanks, Ms. Patel." She stands there two more seconds, and then finally leaves.

"Mom?"

"Oh, Ariel, this is really something . . . your dad *did* collapse," she is almost laughing as she says this.

"What?"

"Remember how the *Godfather* commercial was going to be filmed? We were laughing about it last night at dinner. Your dad was going to have a heart attack like Don Corleone did in the movie. He was going to use the community garden as the site, remember? So I bet the police were talking about it on the air, on the police scanner, maybe keeping people back, making sure traffic kept moving. You know how the community garden is so visible downtown."

Things click into place for me instantly. "Yeah, Mom, it makes sense. Oh God, everyone thinks he *really did* keel over and have a heart attack or something. And all the kids are being so nice to me. Now I'm gonna look like a complete idiot when everyone knows it was all fake." I am talking quietly, away from Ms. Patel, who is pretending to sort papers on the counter by the door.

"Ariel, it was a misunderstanding. No big deal. I am sorry if you were worried. I must admit your call did give me a fright. But everything's okay," she giggles, "and actually, I think it *is* kind of funny."

"Ha." I say it like it is the most unfunny thing I have ever heard. The bell rings, and I say good-bye and hang up. Ms. Patel asks me if everything is okay again. I nod briefly and leave.

I said earlier that Dad spoofs movies to make commercials for Island Sweets. When I was watching *The Godfather* for the fourth time a month or so back, he sat down and watched with me. That's when he came up with the idea for two TV spots.

In the movie, there is this really awful, bloody scene, involving a horse's head in this guy's bed. I will not lie—it's a disturbing sight. But anyway, Dad thought it would be hilarious to recreate the scene using chocolate. In the movie the guy wakes up and is covered in blood, and it's all dramatic as he peels back the silk sheets and finds his horse's head. Then he starts screaming.

Dad did the same scene for his ad, using the exact same silk sheets, and with the same music, but he is covered in chocolate as he dramatically pulls back the covers to reveal a huge pile of tofu and barley and stuff. Health nut foods. Then he screams dramatically like the guy in *The Godfather* did and the voiceover says, "Island Sweets, a *family* tradition since 1922."

The thirty second spot was very popular. I think a few people might have even watched the movie because of it. Not that many kids had seen *The Godfather* before, but I know of at least two kids (okay, so they're M and Nicki, but I bet other kids did too) who were interested in seeing it because of Dad's commercial. Everyone thought it was hysterical, and so Dad decided to follow-up with another spot inspired by *The Godfather*.

This time he would do the death scene of Vito Corleone, the main character in the movie. In the movie, Vito is walking in his tomato garden with his grandson when he has a heart attack. My dad was going to spoof it in the Alameda community vegetable garden, where he was made-up and dressed to look just like Vito did in that scene. The son of a lady who makes custom wedding cakes for Dad's store would play the grandson role. Dad would stroll through the garden and doing his imitation of Marlon Brando, the actor who plays Vito, but when he finally "dies" the "grandson" will turn to the camera and say, "Come into Island Sweets today and try our new Seven-Layer Candied Apples. They're to *die* for!"

That's the commercial dad was filming today. Wow,

this goes to show how much people love to gossip and are so happy, actually eager, to think some tragedy has happened. That's junior high for you. But I guess I got kind of caught-up too. I can't wait to tell M and Nicki about it. I wonder if people will think I was milking it, acting sad and stuff. This is not a great way to start the school year. I can't even believe this is only the first day of school.

I rush out of the office, but everyone is still in class. I will have to wait to tell M and Nicki what happened. I'll be late to my first day of geometry, but Ms. Patel has already given me an excuse slip.

I find the new classroom quickly—I had American history in this room last year—and my new geometry teacher barely looks up as I wave my slip and find a vacant seat. I think over this crazy day, and wonder if the whole year is going to be this full of the un-expected. The earthquake flashes through my mind again, and I wonder why it seems to relate to today's events. Finally, the bell rings and I head to biology, my last class of the day.

Easy "Certain Death"
Orange Chicken*

4 boneless, skinless chicken breasts

1 C. orange juice

2 T. finely chopped orange zest (This is orange peel. You
    can use a vegetable peeler to peel it off, but don't peel
    it so hard that the bitter, white pith comes off too.
    Chop up the peels really small.)

20 to 30 Ritz crackers, crushed into meal (You can put
    them in a ziplock bag, put a towel over the bag and
    whack it with the bottom of a heavy pan until the
    crackers are pulverized. It can be quite therapeutic
    making your own crumbs this way.)

cooking spray

½ C. mustard plus 2 T. orange juice

*Put orange juice, zest, and chicken in a 13x9" baking pan,
cover, and marinate in refrigerator at least a couple hours,
but preferably overnight. Preheat oven to 375°. Remove chicken
from marinade, but allow some of the zest to remain clinging
to it. Put the cracker crumbs in shallow bowl, and dip each
chicken piece into the crumbs. Use your hands to pat and
mash the crackers onto the surface of the chicken so it is*

---

* In *The Godfather*, when an orange appears in a scene (a bowl of
   them, a picture of them on a sign, etc.) it signals that an important
   death scene is about to happen. In fact, Vito is eating an orange
   when he dies in the tomato garden.

well-coated. Wash out and dry your pan (throw out the marinade) and spray it with cooking spray. Put the chicken in the pan and spray the tops of the chicken breasts with cooking spray as well. Bake it for 40 minutes, or until you can prick it with a fork and the liquid that runs out is clear. Let it sit for a few minutes before serving. While it is sitting, combine the mustard and orange juice and use it for dipping sauce when you serve the chicken.

My Casa de Chaos

M and Nicki are coming over soon so we can do
the first day postmortem. (That means "after death,"
like an autopsy. I got the word from watching *CSI*.)
We always hang out at my house because M's mom
seems to get nervous if we're around too much, and
Nicki's house is so quiet and orderly we can't really
cut loose. My house, on the other hand, is generally
kind of messy, usually loud, and frequently crowded
because Ryan's friends are always around. I think my
parents like the chaos.

Another thing is the food. Our house is well-
stocked with snacks and leftovers, and I am constantly
making stuff for people to try. M and Nicki enjoy
my culinary creations, but Ryan and his friends really devour everything. Sixteen-year-old boys eat like
dogs—quantity seems to be the key factor, so I am not

necessarily flattered when they inhale something I've made. I have seen three of them wipe out a family-size bag of tortilla chips, a vat of salsa, and a large package of Oreos in about three minutes.

As soon as the last bell rang, we had reunited next to the eighth-grade lockers. I explained *The Godfather* commercial confusion to them as we walked home.

We pile into my house, a bit out of breath from walking fast. I hang my keys on the little hook by the door as I say, "So you can see how it really would look like Dad keeled over in the community garden. I mean, he really *did*, technically." By now, M and Nicki are both sort of chuckling about it, but shooting me little cautious looks too.

Nicki goes serious as she looks at me and asks, "You're okay now?"

"Yes, no. I *am* totally relieved that Dad's okay, but I can't even fathom my embarrassment level about it all . . . the PA announcement, tripping, my Dad's bad acting . . ." I throw my hand in the air dramatically and collapse onto a chair.

"Air, you're funny—this whole thing is funny," M gives me a playful punch on the shoulder.

"Hilarious," I reply, holding my belly and shrugging my shoulders as though I am cracking up when in fact I am not even smiling.

M rolls her eyes and giggles.

Nicki, sensitive soul that she is, doesn't laugh with

M, but she does smile at me and say, "You really *didn't* know what was going on today. It's not like you made it up for sympathy or something."

"Nope, I didn't." I shrug, fiddling with a loose thread on my cuff. I think about Nicki's reaction, and ask, "Nicki, when you said something earlier about understanding loss, what were you talking about?"

Nicki cuts me off with a forced laugh. It scrapes out of her throat. "God, I don't know. I was trying to be sympathetic is all." She smiles brightly, but I can see that snapping "don't mess with me" flash in her eyes. I know not to push it.

M pipes up, "Well, Nicki *did* almost lose her baby brother."

Nicki looks gratefully at M. "Exactly!"

I say nothing, but I can tell Nicki knows I am still curious.

Nicki goes to the sink to wash her hands and says, "Ariel, this whole thing was just a giant misunderstanding. Maybe M is right, it is a little funny?" She turns off the water and cuts her eyes at me over her shoulder.

My mind flashes to the moment right after the earthquake, that unreal, peaceful silence. Nicki knows that I think she is hiding something. I get up and stand next to her and we both stare out the window. The neighbors have replaced the wind chime that broke in the earthquake, and its tinkling sounds like rain on something metal. I turn away from the window and slump onto a barstool.

M sits next to me as Nicki continues to stare out the window.

Sighing, I admit, "I just feel . . . stupid." I am beginning to see that it really isn't a big deal, but I do feel anxious about it still—like I will become a joke at school because of this whole weird thing with my dad, not to mention the klutz jokes coming my way after tripping in front of the whole school.

"Okay then, what's there to eat?" M gives me a wink and I know we are done talking about it. When M decides to move on from a subject, there's not much more to say.

"Let's chow!" I throw open the fridge door dramatically and do a little cha-cha dance as I pull out tortillas and move the milk jug.

Honestly, I still feel weird and worried. I feel like I did after the earthquake last week. I had been very shaken-up (no pun intended there), maybe even more than M or Nicki, but I had to pop up and act silly right away. I pretended I was unaffected, even though my heart was hammering, my arm throbbed from where the flour canister had hit it, and I felt like I might cry. I didn't, of course. It did make me wonder if I am really as tough as other people think I am, or if I am a big faker.

M and Nicki start talking about going shopping this

weekend. M wonders if she can drag her mom out of the house, and Nicki is talking about going to Michaels to get design ideas for this year's yearbook. My mom is doing laundry in the basement; we hear her muffled "hello" drift up the stairs with the cozy, warm smells of Tide and Downy. Ryan's friend Matt once said, talking while his mouth was stuffed with lemon pound cake, that he loved walking into our house because it always smells like laundry and food. I guess that's true.

I begin rummaging around to see what I can make as a snack for us. I decide to use the tortillas to create something similar to an appetizer recipe I saw on a cooking show. I pull out the blender and begin to assemble it.

"Nicki, look, we're having something blended. Hmm. Smoothies?"

I snap the glass pitcher into the base and shake my head. "Nope."

Nicki props her elbows on the counter. "Please tell me you're not going to put *tortillas* in the blender, Ariel."

I just laugh as I rummage through the condiments in the refrigerator door, pulling out a few random items. "Patience, girls!"

M twirls in circles on her stool, thumping the wall as she makes each turn, her voice getting louder in bursts as she spins past me on the kitchen side. "I feel like this year is going to be harder class-wise."

Nicki snorts delicately, "Maybe you'll actually have to study?"

M comes to a stop on her stool by slapping her palms on the counter in front of Nicki. She gives her signature one-eyebrow-up look. "I studied last year," dramatic pause, "once or twice."

I scrape cream cheese into a bowl and laugh. "M, this *will* be a harder year for you because you have to get *me* through geometry."

As we talk about our classes and I work on the food, I feel myself calming, letting go of this horrible tension I have felt all day.

I put a large serving platter on the breakfast bar. I have sliced the filled, rolled tortillas into pinwheels, and they look kind of elegant. I am pleased. I hope they taste good too. With a little tweaking, this recipe could become a go-to appetizer staple in my recipes binder. I need more appetizer recipes.

I watch M bite into one and chew thoughtfully. "Ariel, these are super good." She shoves the rest in her mouth and bobs her head enthusiastically.

Nicki takes one and delicately pinches off a section. She is always a slow, cautious, tidy eater. She turns her head a bit, contemplating, and says, "Do you have any Tabasco?"

I find the bottle of hot sauce and hand it to Nicki. She shakes out a healthy dollop, takes another teensy bite, and smiles dreamily. "*That* is good."

Nicki eats really, really spicy food. It's one of the things I love about her—the way she gobbles up Thai food that brings most people to their knees, and always sprinkles a whole packet of red pepper flakes on her pizza. Her spicy habit doesn't match her shy, quiet personality, and I find this very pleasing.

We are snacking and gossiping when Mom emerges. She says "Hi" to M and Nicki, not to me. "How was your first day, girls? I guess you heard about my husband's 'heart attack'?" She continues addressing M and Nicki, avoiding me. I guess she's still mad about the bee kit scene.

"Hey, Mom, wanna try these?" I point to the tray on the counter. "Peace offering?" I give her my best "I'm sorry" expression.

I get a long, level look in return, and then she smiles on the left corner of her mouth. A signature Mom expression. It means I am mostly forgiven. "Sure." She pops one in her mouth, whole. "Mmm. Tasty, Ariel. Ryan and Matt will probably inhale the rest of those when they get home from football."

"I made a lot, so that's okay."

Mom ruffles my hair and heads to the front hall. "I have to go get them, but need to stop by the hardware store first. Oh, Mattie? Your mother called and asked me to make sure you are home by 5:30. I think she said that your dad is coming or something . . ." She trails off as she grabs her car keys from a hook by the door.

M looks a bit puzzled, maybe concerned. "Okay, Carolyn," M says. "I'll be sure to take off before then."

The door bangs shut and Nicki and I both turn to stare at M, waiting expectantly for her to speak.

She pops another pinwheel in her mouth and chews loudly. Finally, she says, "I have no idea. My dad isn't supposed to visit until next week. Maybe the message got mixed up or something." She takes another, and carefully drips one drop of Tabasco on it. She chews this one more slowly and shrugs her shoulders.

We spend the rest of the afternoon in my room, laying around and organizing our new binders. Nicki is trying to teach me and M to get more organized, but it is not a successful campaign. Still, with the clean slate of a fresh school year, Nicki is optimistic we will keep "the system"—which involves color-coded, tabbed and labeled binder dividers—in place. Nicki gets a rush from organizing and cleaning. Seriously. I guess we all have our "things."

Nicki leaves before M, and as she rounds the corner outside I see her opening her phone. Again. Another "emergency." I know M thinks I am being suspicious and paranoid, but Nicki is usually not about sneaking and secrets.

M leaves around five, just as my mom, Ryan, and his friend Matt tumble through the door. It gets loud and confusing for a minute with hellos, good-byes, people trying to go both in and out of the front door, our dog

Fiesta barking in excitement, and my mom yelling about Ryan and Matt's dirty sneakers and telling Fiesta to pipe down. Geez, it's la casa de chaos sometimes around here.

I follow M out to the front yard, and we hug on the sidewalk. She promises to call and tell me what's going on.

I go back into the house. The tortilla spirals have already disappeared. In my room, I flip on my PC and begin typing up the recipe and notes for the appetizer I made this afternoon. I stop typing and head to dinner when I hear mom shouting that it's time to chow down. If M hasn't called by after dinner, I am going to call her.

Tortilla Spirals
à la Ariel

6 large flour tortillas

1 package cream cheese, softened

⅓ C. sour cream

½ t. garlic salt

½ t. onion powder

2 T. chopped sun-dried tomatoes (They are usually sold in jars in the produce section. They are totally different-tasting than fresh tomatoes, so don't substitute.)

1 small can chopped olives

⅓ C. chopped nuts—pecans are really good, but pistachios or walnuts or pine nuts would work too

Use a blender or a hand mixer to mix cream cheese, sour cream, onion powder, and garlic salt until fluffy and creamy. Spread equal amounts of cream cheese mixture on each tortilla. Sprinkle all the other ingredients over the cream cheese. Roll each tortilla up as tightly as possible. Using a sharp knife, cut the roll into vertical circles about a quarter inch thick. The slices are pretty spirals, and look nice alone, but a light sprinkling of paprika or perhaps a bit of parsley would look great. Make hot sauce available for dipping.

Devastating News

I tried calling M a bunch of times after dinner, but it kept going to voicemail. Between calls I made a starter for Friendship Bread, which I plan to give to Nicki and M in ten days (that's how long it takes before you can bake with it). I hit redial between each step of the recipe. Making the bread starter is comforting. I also e-mailed M, with an automatic reply to let me know if she had opened it, and so far she hasn't. It's 9:30, and I am seriously tired. This day has been so long. Plus, I didn't get much sleep last night. I need to crash. I am fantasizing about my bed at this point, but I am still worried about M. Once my bread starter is finished and I have cleaned up, I am going to call Nicki to see if she has heard anything.

Nicki answers the phone on the first ring. Her baby brother is probably sleeping.

"Hi, Air," Nicki speaks softly.

"Hey. I know your mom doesn't like us calling after nine, so tell her sorry, but M hasn't called me back. I'm worried. Her dad never *just shows up.*"

"I called her awhile ago and left a message too, but haven't heard anything either."

"It's weird, don't you think?"

Nicki thinks for a few seconds, then replies, "Well, if her dad did come for some reason, they probably went out. You know how he insists that M's mom go out to show she's doing better with the agoraphobia."

"But this late?"

"Yeah, well, I don't know. But we'll find out tomorrow I guess. Look, Ariel, I gotta go, my mom's already irritated about me being on the phone after nine."

"Okay, sorry again. E-mail me if you hear anything though, okay? I'll be up a little bit longer."

"I will. But, Ariel, you know M would call *you* before she called *me* anyway."

This is probably true. While we act like we are all equal friends, the truth is that M and I are closer because we have been best friends since we were little kids, and Nicki moved here the summer before fifth grade. We feel super close to her, but the shared history isn't there yet. And Nicki is such a private person, sometimes it is hard to know what's beyond the sweet part we always see.

Despite the way Nicki keeps to herself, I know she

feels deeply about M and me, and I know it hurts Nicki sometimes when M and I talk about some story from years ago, before we knew Nicki. We try not to do that, but it does happen. Nicki is not the type to make us feel bad about it, though I have seen a look on her face sometimes, when M and I are remembering some funny thing from third grade or whatever. It's a wishing kind of look. She never talks much about her past. It's like her life started when she moved to Alameda.

We hang up and I head to the bathroom for teeth brushing and face washing. I e-mail my mom that I am going to bed. This started last summer as a joke—my mom is usually paying bills and stuff on her computer around the time I go to bed. Last summer, I went in to tell her I was going to bed, and she said she'd be there to tuck me in shortly (yes, she still "tucks me in" but it is something I think *she* needs more than I do, so I keep on letting her even though it is pretty juvenile). Anyway, that night I waited for her, and twenty minutes later she still hadn't come. I felt like I couldn't go to sleep until we did the tuck-in thing, so I e-mailed her that I was *waaaaiiiting.* . . . Thirty seconds later I heard her coming down the hall laughing. She grabbed me in a bear hug and kissed my head about twenty times, apologizing for spacing out and forgetting to come in. She said I should always e-mail her good night. She was kidding, but I started doing it a lot. Now it's still funny, but even better, it works.

Tonight she e-mails me back and says she'll be here in two. I guess M still hasn't read my email. I shut down my PC and crawl into bed. Oh, sweet heaven, my sheets feel delicious.

Mom comes in and kisses my cheek. "Night, honey. Sorry about today. If I embarrassed you, coming in with the bee allergy kit."

I cut her off. "It wasn't the kit, it was that I got called out in front of everyone and I tripped. I know you didn't mean for it to go down like that, Mom. Then the whole 'Dad had a heart attack' story. I just had a weird day."

Mom sits on the side of my bed and nods her head slowly. "Well, you'll always remember the first day of eighth grade. At least it wasn't boring."

I laugh, this is true—it was anything but boring. "Is Dad still at the store?"

"Uh-huh, he's supervising the crew that's refinishing the floor. It'll be midnight by the time he gets home. I told him about the rumor at your school that he *really had* keeled over, and he thought it was hysterical. He said it spoke highly of his acting skills."

I roll my eyes. Dad's commercials could hardly be called acting.

"Tell him I said good night." I snuggle down in my bed, already my eyelids are drooping and I can feel that pleasant heaviness in the back of my skull that tells me I will fall asleep quickly and deeply.

I yawn, and Mom gets up to leave.

"Night, Ariel. Love you."

"Love you too. Oh, Mom?"

She turns back to me, her hand on the door knob. "Hmm?"

"I haven't heard back from M tonight, and I wondered what her mom said when she called today. I mean about her dad."

Mom shrugs her shoulders. "Not much. She just said Mattie needed to come home by 5:30 because her dad was coming. Why? Do you think something's wrong?"

"Yeah . . . no, I don't know. It's just that she didn't ever call or e-mail and she said she would. Her dad usually only shows up for emergencies and birthdays."

"Her mother didn't sound upset or anything. I think everything's fine, Air. You'll talk to her in the morning. Now go to sleep!"

"Night, Mom." She closes the door.

What seems like a minute later she's in my doorway again, the hallway light spilling in a column across the bottom of my bed. I am disoriented and confused. I glance at the clock and see that it's 10:20. I have only been asleep for twenty minutes. My exhaustion must have pulled me under pretty fast. I struggle to my elbows. "Mom?"

"Sweetie, sorry to wake you, but it's Mattie. She's on the phone and she's crying. She wanted me to wake you up. She says it's urgent."

As my eyes adjust and my head clears, I see Mom holding the cordless phone from the living room in her hand.

I sit up and hold out my hand for it. Mom comes over and gives me the phone and a worried look. She just stands there.

"Okay, thanks. Can you close my door on the way out?" She doesn't have to be Sherlock Holmes to figure out I am asking her to leave so I can talk in private.

"Sure. Okay." She leaves reluctantly.

I put the phone to my ear, "M?"

She lets out a fresh sob when she hears my voice. "Ariel? Oh God, Ariel, we're moving!"

"What? Moving?"

"That's why my dad was here tonight. They decided to tell me together. Mom got a job in some remote place way, way up north," M is talking fast and snorting snot and hiccupping all at once. "It's like seven hours away, Air! She didn't tell me about it until now because she didn't want me to get upset before she knew for sure. But now it *is* for sure." She stops and does that kind of crying that sounds like you have asthma.

"Oh, M, I can't believe this!" I can't imagine my life without M by my side at school, or sleeping over on the weekends, or walking the path by the bay, or sitting on a barstool after school cracking jokes while I try out a new recipe. This is devastating. I begin crying too. This is *so* unfair. I hate M's stupid mother with a sudden, furious passion. This will ruin our lives.

"I can go with her to the boonies, or I can go live with Dad if I want," M is taking deeper breaths as she fills in the gaps of her story. "We talked until just a little while ago, and I finally just came in my room and closed the door to call you. I'm talked out about it. I don't know what to do."

M and I stay on the phone until a little after eleven. We e-mail Nicki with the bad news. My mom finally comes in and tells me I have to hang up. I am still crying when I tell my mom the news. She chokes up too. M is practically like a daughter to her.

I don't think I can sleep now, I am too upset. But I fall into a deep, coma-like sleep without any transition.

Friendship Bread

10 DAY STARTER:

  1 envelope dry yeast
  ¼ C. warm water (NOT hot or cold, but warm like the
        temperature that feels good washing your hands)
  3 C. flour
  3 C. sugar
  3 C. milk

THE BREAD:

  1 C. 10 day starter
  1 C. vegetable oil
  2 C. flour
  1 C. sugar
  ½ C. buttermilk
  1 ½ t. baking powder
  ½ t. baking soda
  ¼ t. salt
  3 eggs
  4 t. vanilla

*DAY 1: Don't use metal (bowl or utensils) EVER anywhere in
this recipe—use plastic, ceramic, or glass. Dissolve yeast in
warm water, let it stand 15 minutes. In a separate bowl, mix
1 C. each flour and sugar. Slowly stir in 1 C. milk and yeast*

water, mixing until smooth. Cover with plastic wrap loosely and let it sit on the counter until bubbly. DAYS 2 to 4: stir once with wooden spoon. DAY 5: mix in 1 C. each flour, sugar, milk. DAYS 6 to 9: Stir once a day. DAY 10: add 1 C. each sugar, flour, and milk again. Now you can divide this finished bread starter into three. Keep one-third to make your own bread, and pass along the other two thirds to two friends, along with these instructions, so they can grow their own starter and pass it along to two more people. Some starters have been going for years and years in this way.

To bake the bread, combine all the ingredients listed under "the bread" to make two loaves, or divide in half all the listed ingredients to make one loaf, and mix thoroughly. You can also use half the starter to start the whole process again (but start at day 2, because you already have the first step), making a new batch to divide and give away. Or you can put it in the fridge for up to a week for use later. Just bring it to room temperature before baking with it. Rub the loaf pan(s) with butter and sprinkle sugar on the butter, tapping off extra sugar into sink. Bake at 350° for 55 minutes, or until a toothpick inserted in the middle comes out clean.

A Hard Morning

I look like a glob of dough this morning. Crying before bed has left my eyes swollen, and the skin on my upper lip is splotchy and red from some unmentionable dried stuff that must have been there all night. I jump in the shower, using the five minutes I have to scrub my face with a washcloth and rinse my hair. It's short enough that I can get away with not washing it if I'm tight on time—I just get it wet and then run some gel through it when I get out of the shower. It's spiky and a little edgy when I do this, and even though the red is still very . . . red . . . I think it suits me.

I contemplate M's news as I dress. My eyes well-up again, but I fight it down. I can't cry before school. I feel a tight knot in the pit of my stomach and decide to skip breakfast. As I jam homework, pens, lip gloss, and a black, knit scarf into my backpack, my dad appears in my doorway.

"Morning, Snarfblatt." (Don't ask, it's a nickname from the Disney movie and too ridiculous to define.)

"Hey, Dad." I look up for a second to see him scratching his belly and yawning. Charming.

"Your mother tells me Mattie might be moving." As he speaks he comes in and sits on the edge of my bed.

"Did she also tell you that half of Alameda thought you croaked yesterday?"

"She did. And I think someone in Hollywood is probably searching for me as we speak, having heard about my incredible acting talent."

His joking annoys me. And his fat belly poking out of his pajama top annoys me. Also that he is lounging on my bed.

"Dad, I gotta get over to M's house now." I swing my backpack onto one shoulder and make my way to the door.

He stands up quickly and follows me. As we walk down the hallway, he reaches out and pulls me backward by a backpack strap, circling his arms around my neck so I am pinned. My irritation hits a new high.

"Dad! I gotta go! Knock it off!"

He just laughs, and spins me to face him. "Oh now, is my princess in a hurry?"

I just glare.

He lets go of me and takes a step back. "I was just

kidding, hon. Your mom said you had such a hard day yesterday, and I got home so late, we couldn't talk. Well, I just wanted to say I am sorry about M—and that I love you." He ruffles my hair, and then makes a face of horror as he rubs his now hair-gelled hand on his pajama pants.

I can't help laughing just a tiny bit at this. That's the thing about Dad. Half the time he embarrasses and irritates me and the other half he is this great, solid force of humor and support.

"Okay, Dad." I peck his cheek.

"Want to make those oven ribs this weekend?" he asks as I head to the front door.

"Really? Okay, sure! That would be fantastic, Dad. I've only waited *forever* for this!"

"But you can never reveal my secret rib technique, Ariel. It must stay in the family." He is using his fake, raspy *Godfather* voice.

"I swear. But I gotta run . . . bye, Dad!" I let the door bang shut as I tromp down the steps.

As I walk the few blocks to M's I think about the ribs. It keeps me from obsessing about M for the moment. I have been asking my dad to show me his "secret" rib technique for practically a year now, and he has taunted me by holding out on me.

What happened is this: last Super Bowl Sunday my parents were having the usual party we have every year. My dad loves barbecuing, and he actually rents an extra-large grill to use for the skewers of teriyaki chicken, beef brochettes, oysters in the shell from Half Moon Bay, and his famous, legendary, world-changing baby back ribs (and those are actual descriptions people have used to express their reactions to these ribs).

Well, last year the rented grill broke, and they couldn't get a replacement in time for Dad to start cooking the ribs. The ribs have to cook for six hours or so. When the replacement grill showed up about noon, Dad had already started the ribs in the oven. I remember comforting him and telling him people would understand if they weren't as good this year. He told me not to tell anyone about the ribs, and we'd just see if anyone noticed a difference.

Long story short, they didn't. I didn't. The short ribs had the slightly charred, smoky flavor of long, low-heat grilling. The meat practically fell off the bones, as usual. I didn't know how he did it in the oven. Ever since then I have asked him to show me, but he's held out. Until now. As I climb the cracked steps to M's front door I realize he wanted to give me something this morning, and the promised sharing of the rib secret is his gift. It's his apology and comfort.

M hears me on the front porch and swings the door open. She looks pale and serious as she pulls me through the door and hugs me hard. I hug her back. Her mom comes out of the kitchen and gives me a bright, fake smile.

"We'll get going as soon as Nicki gets here," she speaks in a forced-normal voice.

"We're going to wait outside," M speaks to her mother in a frosty tone as she pulls me back out the front door.

We sit on the bottom step. I ask her, "So is it really going to happen? You moving?"

I can tell M has cried so much she's emptied out right now—that's how her voice sounds as she speaks. "My mother signed a work contract a week ago. Our house is going up for sale next week."

Just then Nicki comes around the corner and breaks into a little trot when she sees us waiting outside. M's mom must have been watching from the window because she comes right out and says, "Let's go, girls."

It is weirdly quiet in the car. Normally we are all chatting, interrupting each other, trying to remember what we forgot to pack, and checking our hair one last time. Today we are mute. M's mom tries to make conversation a couple of times on the short drive to school, but it falls flat. Nothing is said about the move. We get out quickly and M's mom drives off. No air kisses to catch today.

There's no time to talk before homeroom. Nicki and I both give M a quick hug before we split up for the morning. M is going to tell us the whole story at lunch. I really want to know exactly what is going to happen, but I am also dreading it.

Secret Oven
Baby Back Ribs

2 racks baby back ribs
½ C. spice rub (any kind of spice rub for meat will work—
    you can find them on the spice aisle)
1 bottle your favorite BBQ sauce
⅓ C. honey
1 t. hot paprika OR 1 t. sweet paprika plus ½ t. cayenne
    pepper
4 T. liquid smoke (in bottles in the spice aisle)

*Rinse ribs and cut into smaller racks of about 5 ribs each.
Rub the "mini-racks" all over with the spice rub, making sure
to cover the ends. Put them in a huge ziplock bag and let
them sit in the fridge at least a day, but up to three days. The
longer they sit in the spice rub, the more intense the flavor. On
cooking day, remove them from the fridge for an hour before
cooking. Preheat oven to 475°. Line two roasting or jellyroll
pans with tinfoil. Pour water into the bottom of the pans as
full as you can, but not so full that you will spill when you put
the pans into the oven. Add 2 T. liquid smoke to the water in
each pan. Put a cooling rack over the water-filled pans and
arrange the ribs in a single layer on the racks. Put the pans
in the oven and turn the temperature down to 275°—don't
open the oven door for at least an hour. Meanwhile, make the
basting sauce by mixing the bottled sauce with the honey and
spices. Cook the ribs for about 6 hours, turning them over and
switching the pan positions on the racks in the oven every hour*

or so. In the last hour, use a brush to baste the ribs with the sauce, making thin, even coats on all surfaces, and turning them frequently. They are done when the meat is pulling away from the bones on the ends and they are just starting to burn a tiny bit on the edges. Pile them on a big platter and cover them with several layers of newspaper. Let them sit 20 minutes, and then cut them into individual ribs for eating.

The INCREDIBLE IDEA Is Born

By lunchtime I realize that my brief moment basking in the attention and kindness of my fellow middle schoolers was just that—a moment. I get a couple of eye rolls in the hallway, but mostly everyone is back to ignoring me. Well, except the boys, who are back to staring at me, but they aren't exactly looking at my face, so that is essentially another kind of being ignored. Typical and familiar.

It's finally lunchtime. M and Nicki are already at our table. M's going to give us all the horrible details about moving. I have been feeling sick with dread all morning. A tiny part of me thinks she won't really move. She just can't *leave* us. It's unfathomable.

I have a little container of fettuccine carbonara from dinner last night. It's one of my mom's go-to recipes. It does involve a mix, which I am generally against, but for a fast meal it is pretty good. Even foodie families like mine have to have a few "quick and dirty" meals (that's what Dad calls them) when life gets too busy.

"Okay, M, spill." I slurp a cold noodle off my plastic spoon and wait.

"I have been so worried all morning," Nicki is peeling an orange very slowly, so that the peel stays in one long spiral. "I keep thinking this isn't real. You just can't leave Alameda, leave us."

M sighs and her shoulders slump. I notice she has no lunch.

"Where's your lunch?" I ask her. Current drama aside, the girl's gotta eat.

"I forgot to pack anything," M shrugs, uncaring, "I have no appetite anyway."

Nicki rips her peeled orange in half and hands one half it to M, who tears off a segment and eats it mechanically. I rummage around in my backpack and come up with a fork. It is not exactly clean, but it'll do. I stab it into the noodles and scoot the container toward M. She idly winds a noodle around the grungy fork, playing with it, not eating.

"Thanks, guys, but I am seriously not hungry." As she says this she shoves another orange segment in her mouth. Okay then. I see the purplish shadows beneath her eyes and the little, sore-looking cracks around her lips. M is in bad shape.

"Okay, but take as much as you want, M. You

should eat." Mother Nicki pats M on the back lightly and pushes the rest of her lunch toward M.

M waves her away. "All morning I kept thinking about last times. Like, 'This is the last time I'll be here for a fire drill,' or 'This is the last time I'll be here for school pictures'—stuff like that." M's voice is almost dreamy. I know it is exhaustion and hunger that make her sound so frail.

"So your mom got a job?" I am prompting her, I need details. I don't think she realizes that Nicki and I still know next to nothing about this whole thing.

"Yep, in a town called Crescent City. It's way, way up north, right by the Oregon border. There's this huge prison there called Pelican Bay. My dad says they keep the worst criminals there. It's called a Supermax prison because the guys there are so dangerous. Isn't that charming?"

"But what's that got to do with anything?" Nicki gives voice to my own confusion.

"That's where the job is. Mom is going to be working in an office job at the prison. It has something to do with tracking and billing for the prisoners' medical care."

"I thought your mom liked working from home. I mean with her . . . problems." I am trying to be delicate. M can be a little prickly about her mom's weirdness. Understandably.

"Apparently my parents have been struggling

for awhile with money. Since the divorce actually. My mom was too messed up to get a job out of the house, and so they had to take out an extra loan on the Alameda house. Mom's work at home doesn't make enough money to pay all these house bills, plus there aren't any benefits, like insurance and stuff. Mom's therapy and her meds have helped enough to make her feel like she can work in a real job now. She started looking over the summer and found this prison thing."

"Couldn't she work somewhere around here?" I interrupt to ask.

"I said that too, Air. She said it's just too expensive here, and moving makes sense. She wants a fresh start, and it doesn't seem to matter that I don't want any kind of new start because I like it here. She says Crescent City is really small and clean and beautiful. Like I *care* that there're redwood trees and cool lighthouses." M is cycling from defeated and sad to mad.

"My dad says it's the perfect solution. Mom and I can buy a bigger house there, and it'll cost less. They can pay off all these huge debts. They went on and on about salaries, pensions, saving for my college and blah, blah, blah. They made working for a prison sound like winning the lottery. Mom is all excited to have her 'fresh start,' and they both went on and on about how I can visit here in the summer, how I'll adjust, make new friends. That kind of total crap." M tears the remaining orange savagely and bites into a segment like she's ripping its head off.

She keeps talking even though she hasn't swallowed the orange, and little flecks fly out as she continues. "They also said they think the Bay Area isn't *wholesome*, and that I'll be better off in a smaller place, a place where things don't move so fast." She finally swallows and shakes her head in disbelief. "Can you even believe this? I mean, I get great grades, never get in trouble . . . what exactly is *unwholesome* about here, about me here?"

"It's totally unfair, M," I tell her, and I mean it. This whole thing is stunning. Nicki adds, "I had to move last year, so I know how you feel, M."

"But, Nicki, you said *we* were the best friends you ever had. That in North Fork you had lots of friends, but not like us. And you always wanted to move away, to get out from underneath all those cousins," M replies.

Nicki looks down and twirls a piece of her hair. I see her fist knot under the table and her back becomes very stiff. It's almost as if M's remark has angered Nicki. She takes a deep breath, seems to decide something, and turns to M.

Nicki's voice is controlled and she looks hard at M. "I did leave some family, some people, I liked, loved, *and* some good friends. I left more than you know, so don't act like you've cornered the market on sucky moves."

M and I are both so surprised to see Nicki get like this. We are silent.

Nicki seems to catch herself and looks up embarrassed. She takes a breath and gives a little "whatever" shrug as she continues. "Sorry, M. I am not saying it's the same for you as it was for me. Just that I can relate to the feeling of having your whole world change."

"What happened, Nicki?" M asks her gently.

Nicki gives her a funny look. "Nothing *happened*. I just meant, you know, that I could understand how much it stinks to get uprooted." Nicki's voice has returned to its normally soft range. "This isn't about *me*, Mattie, and I didn't mean it to be. I am just so sad for you. For us."

Nicki's outburst forgiven, M reaches over and squeezes Nicki's fingers. "Sorry, Nick, sorry. I know it probably sucked for you too, I am just so . . . so . . ." she shakes her head in frustration, unable to find a mere word to suit this situation. She settles for making an angry grunting noise in the back of her throat.

"You said maybe you could live with your dad in Sacramento?" I ask her.

"Like *that* would be a solution. I can't imagine living there. Or with him." More snorting.

I feel so terrible for M; this is all utterly unjust. "It's awful being at the total mercy of our parents," I was thinking this earlier, and now I tell my friends. "It's like we have no say-so in our own lives. Not really. If they want to move us like Monopoly pieces, they can."

M nods vigorously. "Exactly, Air. I hate being a kid right now more than anything. It's not like there's anything I can do to stop this."

Nicki chimes in, "And they always say it's for our own good, as though we are infants incapable of knowing *for ourselves* what is good for us." Her voice is angrier than I have heard it before.

We are all quiet for a minute, thinking, presumably, about the general lack of power any of us really has.

And that's when I get an idea. It is a whopper of a solution. It's genius! I jump up so fast I hit my elbow on the table, but I don't care. I know what we can do!

Quick and Dirty
Fettuccine Carbonara

1 lb fettuccine (or any kind of pasta you want)

1 C. chopped prosciutto or ham

1 small bag frozen green peas (If you hate peas, like Nicki,
    you can leave them out, or substitute another sweet
    veggie, like carrot or red bell pepper, in its place.)

1 envelope dry fettuccine Alfredo sauce mix

½ t. nutmeg

*Thaw peas in microwave according to package instructions.
Mix prosciutto or ham into drained peas. Cook pasta
according to package instructions. While pasta cooks, make
Alfredo sauce according to packet directions. Mix in the
peas and ham and the nutmeg to the finished sauce. Drain
pasta and mix the noodles and sauce in a big bowl until well
combined. Serve with parmesan cheese to sprinkle on top.*

A Definite Maybe

I am not inclined to run anywhere. In PE I wear two
sports bras to even walk fast, but today I am jogging
home. Nicki and M egged me on right after last bell,
saying, "Run, Air, hurry. Call us as soon as you know!"

And so now I am trotting along the sidewalk, trying to ignore the bouncing going on in the front and
the pain of about twenty pounds of books in my backpack slamming into my back. I stomp up the steps,
already calling for my mom before I am even through
the door.

She comes out of the kitchen, wiping her hands on
a dish cloth. "Ariel, geez, what's up? Were you chased
home by wolves?"

"Very . . . funny, Mom." I take a couple of deep
breaths and feel my heartbeat slow down a little. My
heart hasn't worked this hard since the scare of the

earthquake. And, just like that day, things are getting shaken up and shifted around again.

"Well?" she waits expectantly, twirling the dishtowel around her wrist.

"Mom, you know how M has to move, right?"

Mom nods.

"You know she is practically my *sister.* I mean she's like a *daughter* to you, too."

Mom leans against the doorframe and crosses her arms. "Where are you going with this, Ariel?"

"Well, you know this is our last year before high school. It's *such* an important year for us. I can't imagine losing M *now* . . ."

Mom interrupts me, "For the love of God, Ariel, get to your point!"

I walk over to the couch and sit down next to Mom. I take her hand and give her my best sincere look. "Mom, she could live here, with us! Just for the rest of the year." I speak quickly, anxious to make my case before she can say no. "She's here all the time anyway, and you always say she's already part of the family. Mom, I *know* it could work!"

Mom listens intently. She knots the dishtowel into a little turban for her fist and stares at it as she asks, "I assume you, Nicki, and M came up with this 'solution' together?"

"Well, it was my idea actually, but right away they could see how perfect it was too."

"And don't you think Mattie's parents might not be thrilled with this plan?"

"Her dad will basically do what her mom says, and we think her mom will give into it. You know, wanting what is best for M and all that." My parents are always saying they want what's best for us, after all.

"Because, Mom, seriously, M moving to some podunk town that's way the heck up the coast is *not* what is best."

Mom is still staring at the dishtowel. All she says is, "Hmmm."

"Well, what do you think?" I ask, when she still doesn't say anything.

"I think her mother is not going to agree to this, Ariel. That's what. I would never allow you to live elsewhere for months and months."

I interrupt her, "But, Mom, Ms. Connor isn't *you.* She could get all settled in up there herself, and M could finish junior high here, like she should. Then, in the summer, M could move there and have some free time to adjust before starting high school. It's *ideal.*" I think I have hit every point Nicki, M, and I came up with when we were planning the "presentations." I imagine M, a few blocks away, sitting on her couch with her mom having a very similar talk.

"You would have to share your room."

"Does that mean you're saying yes?" I try to look so grateful and happy that she wouldn't dare shatter my soul with any other answer. Ask any kid, the manipulative look is a power tool.

"No, it does *not* mean yes, and don't give me that look."

Oops, guess I overdid it a little. "A maybe-yes?"

"It's a maybe-*maybe*, Air. This is a big thing you guys are asking. I really don't think Mattie's parents will be on board, frankly, and of course your dad and I need to talk it over and consider it in terms of our family. And then there's the impact on your brother . . ."

I cut her off. "Ryan gets along fine with her, he won't care."

"That may be the case, but there are just a lot of issues to consider."

"But you think there's a definite possibility, right?"

Mom laughs, "Oh, Ariel, if you decide not to be a chef you'd make a great lawyer. Go ahead, go call them and tell them it's a definite maybe. I imagine Mattie is also presenting this campaign to her mother, so go see what she says. We'll discuss it when our family is all together at dinner tonight."

I peck Mom on the cheek. "Thanks, Mom, I really do think this can work. I am *so* excited."

"Don't get too excited. This is by no means a done deal, Air. It is on the table for discussion at this point, nothing more, nothing less."

"I know. But I am hopeful." I clasp my hands

together at my heart and flutter my eyelashes. I can't help it; I have a corny gene that will not be repressed.

"Can I hope," my mother flutters her own eyelashes in an exaggeration of me, "that you will make that couscous salad, the Greek one with the feta, to go with the lemon chicken I am making for dinner?"

"Sure, Mom, after I call the girls and get my math done. I would love to. We can talk about talking to Dad then."

"Okay, Ariel, but like I said, we'll see about all this." Mom gets up and heads back into the kitchen, pausing in the entryway to turn back. "Be careful about being too hopeful, okay, honey? All three of you."

I give her a little aye-aye salute and head for my room to call M.

Couscous Salad
with Optimistic Olives
and Fearless Feta

Salad:

1 box couscous

¼ C. kalamata olives roughly chopped (or just use black or
green olives if you don't have these Greek ones)

1 sm. package feta cheese, crumbled

½ red or orange bell pepper, diced

½ C. fresh parsley chopped (omit if you don't have fresh
parsley—it's still good without it)

Dressing:

2 T. olive oil

2 T. red wine or apple cider vinegar

1 T. lemon juice

1 t. sugar

1 T. fresh oregano chopped, or ½ t. dried oregano

salt and pepper

*Cook couscous according to directions on box, leave lid on and
set aside when it's done cooking, and chop everything while it
sits. Dump couscous into a bowl and stir it around, separating
the clumps and letting it cool off somewhat. Mix the salad
ingredients. Mix the dressing ingredients in a small bowl
with a whisk until well blended to make dressing. Pour over
couscous salad and refrigerate until ready to eat.*

Operation Save M is Underway

I am having a hard time focusing in history this morning. My mind keeps returning to little snippets of conversation from last night and replaying them. I realize we are about to have a pop quiz on the events leading up to World War II, and my chances of performing well are slim at best. Darn it! That was one of the "parental points of concern" (PPC's—as we had labeled them on our list yesterday) that M and I wouldn't do as well in school if she came to live with us. Yesterday, when we were hatching this whole idea, we made up the list of PPC's we thought they'd use to shoot us down. We had guessed that grades would be a big PPC, and so we were ready to tell them how the opposite would be true. We would have live-in study partners in each other, allowing us to do even better in school. But now I am, unfortunately, about to bomb this quiz and arouse parental concern.

Why didn't I pay more attention to the history reading last night? Mr. Kerrigan has told us repeatedly that he loves pop quizzes, and I should have been prepared. Especially right now, when little stuff will really get noticed. I did do the reading last night, technically, but I was also eavesdropping on my mother's phone conversation at the same time. It was one of those weird brain things where you are actually reading something without taking it in at all because you are focusing on something else entirely. I got to the end of the chapter and couldn't remember even one tiny thing about the passage.

I breathe deeply and resolve—promise myself in fact—not to let this happen again. But then I'm not usually distracted from my reading by anything as interesting as the conversation that happened last night.

Basically, here's what happened: I called M right after I talked to my mom, and M's mom had said the same thing my mom did—she didn't say no, but she was pretty down on it actually being realistic. She felt sure my parents would never agree to such a plan, and that it was way too big a thing to ask of them. M and I laughed about this—both sets of parents looking to the other to shut down the possibility of M coming to live with us. M's mom was going to talk to her dad, and I had to go eat dinner with my family to talk about it, so we agreed to get on our computers later, with Nicki too, and IM about it.

My mom laid it all out quickly, as we ate. My dad said it was up to my mom, that he thought maybe Mattie might enjoy being part of a real family. (My mom shushed him when he said that. Dad is just really honest sometimes, but maybe not always perfectly sensitive.) I figured he would leave it up to Mom.

It was Ryan's reaction that startled me. I know Ryan tolerates M, maybe even thinks she's okay most of the time. She's been a fixture at our house for so many years that he is certainly used to her. I anticipated Ryan would be more or less neutral, or maybe he would make a few demands about not giving up more bathroom cabinet space or limiting shower length. I thought maybe he'd demand something or work an angle. Instead, he argued quite well that M should be invited to come and stay here. He told my parents, and more convincingly than I could have, how important the last year before high school is, both academically and socially. He talked about how everything changes in high school. He wolfed down couscous, gulped milk, and chomped his way through three pieces of chicken, all the while making my case for me.

It confused me. Why was he so worried all of a sudden about M or me? But mostly, I felt grateful to him. I could tell my parents were taking him seriously and slowly falling into the 'yes' camp. By the end of dinner

Mom and Dad had agreed, cautiously, to consider it seriously.

After dinner I IM'd M and told her all about it. She said her mother had cried and said a bunch of stuff about being a bad mother, and M had had to comfort her and make her realize this request wasn't personal. She said she felt really bad thinking about her mom all alone in a new place, and had to remind herself that it was her mom's own fault for deciding to move like this. So finally M and her mother called M's dad and talked to him on speakerphone, and he said he thought it was a bad idea, but would not interfere if M's mom decided otherwise.

We finally agreed that our moms should talk, and right away, while the momentum of this whole thing was going so strong. I said I'd get my mom to call M's mom. My mom is the type to resolve and settle things right away, and she's not even remotely shy, so she was the obvious choice to make the call. M's mom is the opposite and could probably not be trusted to actually pick up the phone.

I headed back to the kitchen after logging off the computer, and heard the usual background noises of clanking dishes and water mixing in with the rise and fall of Mom and Dad talking. Sometimes their conversations get loud, to compete with the noisy cleanup, and sometimes they bend their heads together, side by side at the sink, and speak so softly they are almost whispering. They always do dishes and talk like that after dinner. In fact, since I was a little kid I have eavesdropped as much as possible during their dish talks.

Over the years I have secretly learned about getting our dog, Fiesta, for Christmas, that we were going to go on a cruise with my grandma, and that my mother thinks our shy neighbor, Mr. Tory, has a crush on M's Aunt Winda. All bits of information I was not meant to hear. Ryan and I are supposed to be doing homework right after dinner, but we both find lots of reasons to hang around the kitchen and listen.

I knew they were talking about M. I'm sure they were analyzing me, and Ryan, and probably M's somewhat crazy mother and father. They were speaking too softly for me to hear them; their heads bent so close together that Mom's hair was falling over Dad's ear.

I sauntered in, acting casual, and announced, "I've been instant messaging with M, and her mom didn't say no."

They turned to me, waiting for more. My dad raised one eyebrow and remarked, "I guess that's your way of saying she didn't say yes either?"

"She's like you guys. You know, considering it."

A look passed between my parents. I could tell they already knew how this was going to go down. They are such schemers. "We thought it would be best if we all got together in person," Mom said, "to hash it all out.

M and her mother, all of us. We thought we'd invite them to lunch this weekend."

It was only Tuesday, so the weekend was a mile away. I didn't want everyone to over-think this. Adults thinking a lot usually leads to "no" in my experience. I made my appeal. "Why not sooner? I mean, so we aren't *tortured* waiting four days to see how our *whole lives* are going to go here!"

Dad rolled his eyes and said, "Nice drama, Snarfblatt, but we want to have a few days to chew on all this. Mattie's mom probably needs some time too."

I could tell their minds were made up and I wouldn't be able to move up the get-together. Besides, the fact that the parents were actually considering this in a serious way was spectacular. We would all just have to live with the stress of waiting. I bet I will get pimples on my chin because of this stress. That happens to me.

"Will you call and set it up?" I asked Mom.

"Yep. Now enough already, Air, don't you have homework to finish before bed?"

So that's when I headed off to read history. Only I was listening to Mom make the call, talking to M first and then M's mother. I heard enough to know this thing might really happen. We are meeting on Saturday at a restaurant in Jack London Square.

Ryan came in after that and begged me to make him a fried egg sandwich. I make a killer fried egg sandwich. I have no idea how he could be hungry after the huge pile of food he ate at dinner. Normally I would have teased him a little, and I might or might not have made the requested sandwich for him, but last night I would have cooked him ten sandwiches if he'd asked me to. I owe him for talking to Mom and Dad like he did. He knows it too. I still don't get it, but I am grateful.

By the time I went to bed, I was too wiped out to reread the history chapter. Now I'm unprepared. I hunker down in my chair, carefully filling in my name and the date before looking over the questions on the quiz. Hopefully I remember more than I think I do.

Ariel's Excellent
Fried Egg Sandwich

2 pieces of bread
butter
1 egg
salt and pepper
1 slice cheddar cheese
1 slice tomato

Melt a small amount of butter in a skillet on medium heat.
Crack egg into hot skillet and cook it "over medium" (until
the white part is totally cooked but the yolk is still slightly
runny). If runny yolk makes you feel ill, as it does Nicki, you
can cook your egg "over hard" by flipping it over with a spatula
and cooking it until the yolk is solid. Lightly butter both
sides of the bread. When your egg is cooked, put it on one of
the buttered pieces of bread, put the cheese on top of the egg,
and the tomato slice on top of the cheese. Salt and pepper
the tomato and top it with the other piece of bread. Cook the
sandwich, turning it over a time or two with your spatula,
until it is golden and the cheese inside is melted.

The Big Lunch

The rest of this week went by faster than I thought it would. School is harder this year, and I need to study almost two hours each night to keep up. I get to retake my history quiz (which, unsurprisingly, I failed), and I have been knocking myself out preparing for that. The retest will be harder—that's Mr. Kerrigan's whole philosophy, his way of teaching us a lesson. If you flunk you can take a makeup test, but it will be a harder, longer test, and the grade you get on it will replace the original grade even if it is worse. The guy is an evil genius, though I have to admit that I know every stupid fact about World War II by now.

Nicki says she also feels a bit beaten down this year with all the studying. She does seem to have much less free time than last year, always saying she needs to get home to study. She spent so much time making our school's yearbook last year, and I can tell she wants to be even more involved this year. Only M, who is naturally good at school, complains about too much free time. We don't have the time to walk on the trails around the bay as much as we used to. Only M is regularly free after school.

Nicki is really into tennis and has lessons twice a week after school. At home, she spends a lot of time on the phone. I know this because they don't have call waiting and their line is busy a lot. She says she has a lot of cousins to keep up with, but never gets more specific than that.

I play piano and my weekly lesson is on a different day than Nicki's tennis. I also work one afternoon a week after school reshelving books in the public library. Right there that's four days of the week we can't get together. And, of course, I need to spend a lot of time in the kitchen, looking at recipes, studying various techniques, watching cooking shows.

People, even M and Nicki sometimes, see my cooking as a hobby, but I know it will be my career. I could read and study and experiment with food for a hundred years and I wouldn't have cracked the surface of all there is to learn. All the spices, cooking methods, ethnicities . . . food—making it, tasting it, presenting it, experimenting with it, serving it is, well, limitless. So I need a good chunk of time for myself in this area.

M doesn't have a passion like cooking or yearbook.

She doesn't play a sport or musical instrument or volunteer anywhere. She doesn't belong to any clubs at school. She doesn't really even have hobbies. Well, she is trying to rebuild her pig collection (long story) by trawling eBay and Amazon Marketplace, but that's about it hobby-wise, and that isn't really a huge deal. She also needs less time to study. Her mom never takes her anywhere on the weekends, and her dad shows up here and there but it's always dinner out and that's about it. Nicki and I do weekend trips, evening concerts and movies and that kind of thing with our families, while M seems to be home a lot.

M is bored, I think, and understandably. But Nicki and I just can't do the long walks like we used to. I feel bad about it, and I have said so to M once or twice, but she just waves her hand, or snorts and says it's all cool. If she comes to live with us it'll be better for her. I know how my parents are, and they'll get her interested in more things, and she'll go out more with us. She can help me study and be around for sampling my food portfolio as I continue to build it. I am so excited about it, about how great it will be for her, and for me. I can't stand this waiting to see if our parents will agree.

At long last it's Saturday—finally time for our big lunch. I have thought about it so much that I feel almost sick with anticipation. I put extra gel in my hair and wear mascara. My parents, Ryan, and I are taking the ferry from Alameda to Oakland. It would only take twenty minutes to drive there, but we decided to take the ferry because it's just a nice way to travel. M and her mother are going to drive and meet us there. Her mother is not interested in the big open space of the ferry trip. It is obvious, just from hearing M talk, that her mom sees any outing as a task, never a pleasure.

We leave the house with barely enough time to make it out to the ferry terminal. Fiesta runs out the door at the last minute and there's the usual Solomon family dog dance—as Mom calls it—where we all use fake, baby voices and false promises of dog treats to con Fiesta out of the neighbor's flower bed. Finally my dad gets him by the collar from behind and drags him back inside. And we're off.

In the car we talk loudly and interrupt each other. Ryan repeatedly drives his elbow into my thigh when I make comments he does not care for, mostly involving girls. I squeal "ow" and my dad says "Ryaaaaan" but he doesn't actually sound even remotely worried that my thigh muscle is being bludgeoned by Ryan's pointy elbow. My parents hold hands on the gear shift. Dad steers with one hand and Mom has her head tilted back on the seat. It feels almost like we are going to a party, which I think is a sign that things will work out.

The ferry is already there when we pull into the parking lot. We pile out quickly, and all of us break into a run when the blaring horn sounds to announce that the ferry is about to leave. We climb the steep inside steps and come out on the top of the catamaran. It is windy and cold but sunny, slightly smelly and very clear. The hulking cargo loaders lining the narrow passageway to Oakland look like giant metal monsters about to bend down and eat the ships below them. The ships themselves are impossibly huge. People on their decks look about as big as ants on a car. The ships are enormous, floating cities with strange, foreign names and colorful alphabets painted on their sides.

A group of Japanese tourists sits across from our family. They stare in awe at the ships, cargo loaders, passing sailboats, and San Francisco, which glitters in the distance. They fuss with the timer on a camera. Dad offers to take their picture. He takes three. One of the little kids, can't be more than seven, is pointing to Dad and talking really fast.

When dad gives back the camera, the mom, in an accent, says to Dad, "You do commercial in the television, no? *Godfather*? Shop of candy? My son, he says you are same man."

Dad beams. "That's me, yes ma'am. Stop into the shop, it's right on Park in Alameda, and I'll give you a free truffle!"

The woman beams back. I don't know if she knows what a truffle is. The little boy stares shyly at Dad as though he were a famous movie star.

The rest of the trip, all ten minutes, is over quickly. The Japanese family goes downstairs. Ryan ogles the girl who collects the tickets, and Mom closes her eyes and rests her head on the back of the bench, enjoying the bright sunlight. I am watching the shadow of my torso, strangely distorted into something very long and thin, against the riveted, metal side of the deck. My chest is barely visible in the silhouette. If only. But still, it is one of those little perfect spots of time when life is so . . . I don't know, aligned.

We make our way off the ferry and into the restaurant about ten minutes early. M's not here yet. My parents let us order drinks and appetizers. Ryan chooses nachos, predictably (they are a volume choice), and I opt for a cold shrimp plate with fried sage leaves. I never thought of frying sage leaves, and I am intrigued, so naturally I have to order it. Ryan makes gagging noises. Ape.

M and her mother come in just as the appetizers are served. My parents stand up and our mothers hug. It is awkward. My dad hugs M briefly and gives her mom a pat on the back. Again, awkward. Ryan inhales nachos and makes some sort of grunting hello noise. M scoots into the booth next to me. We squeeze hands under the table. M has faint circles of sweat showing through her shirt under the arms, and she is wearing too much eyeliner. She looks pale and tired. I feel so bad for her.

Awkward continues to be the key word as my dad pushes Ryan's plate of nachos, which have been reduced to a small pile of naked tortilla chips and a blob of refried beans floating in a puddle of sour cream, toward M's mom. Polite no-thank-yous fire back and forth. I offer shrimp, but the fried sage leaves look like some rare insect that met up with a fry cooker and got crumbled over the little curlicued shrimp bodies. I decide against trying to get them to try it, explaining how good it tastes. Everyone is painfully tense here.

Finally, my mother, bless her, gets to it. We were all about to melt down under this weirdly tense vibe. She bites a wilted chip and says with false cheer, "I hear Crescent City is beautiful."

M's mom smiles gratefully. She seems so pathetic— thin and worn-out. "I haven't actually been there yet, but the internet pictures look quite lovely."

Silence again. Not comfortable.

Ryan chimes in. "That prison is *tough.* I mean, I read that the guys there are so dangerous that the guards can shoot them if they even fight in the yard." He bobs his head enthusiastically, scraping the last chip through the creamy brown sludge on the nacho plate. "Man, that is awesome!"

M's mom shifts around uncomfortably on the booth seat. The vinyl makes a little whining noise, and she is clearly embarrassed. It is the kind of noise that might be construed as a fart, but, of course, everyone pretends not to have heard it.

She clears her throat and turns to Ryan. "Well, um,

I don't know about all that. My job will not involve the inmates. Well, not the inmates in person. Just billing and paperwork involving them." She shakes her head and gives Ryan a tight smile.

My dad pipes up, passing out the pile of menus to everyone as he says, "Shall we order?"

He obviously means before we talk about what we came here to talk about. This small talk feels so fake when we are all just waiting to get into the real conversation. It feels the same way as when I am waiting my turn to play for a piano recital. I just want to get to it already.

Finally, we have all ordered. I feel my mother shift a bit, sort of lean into the table and square her shoulders, and I know *it* is about to begin: *the discussion.*

"Well, Ariel has certainly lobbied hard for getting Mattie to stay with us," Mom's tone is carefully light and a bit exploratory. I know she is trying really hard to be delicate. She's good at this sort of thing.

M chimes in, "Mom, tell her what you said on the way over here."

Everyone waits politely.

"I said it was too much to ask of you, and too much to accept even if you agree to this idea." Her mom is looking down at the table, but her voice sounds very assured. She is not wavery-sounding about this.

M huffs out a frustrated breath and says to my mom, "I *told* her that she should trust me more. I mean if you and Mr. Solomon said okay to this, I would, of course, help out, be easy. I'd be so grateful!"

My dad, sitting on M's other side, briefly places his hand on her shoulder and smiles at her. "We know, Mattie, we love having you, hon. But your mother's probably got a lot of reasons to be against this . . ."

M interrupts. "If you tell her it *really is* okay, then she might come around." M turns to Dad, and I can see she is about to cry, "I *can't* move away like this, not now. Please!" A tear sneaks out and runs down her cheek, smearing her eyeliner and making her look completely pathetic.

I hear Dad take a deep breath and exhale very slowly. He pats M's hand and says, to her mom, "Carolyn and I would be happy to have Mattie stay with us through the end of the school year. That said, it is obviously a big decision for you, and we completely understand your not wanting to be apart from her like that."

Just then the food comes, and everyone goes quiet as the waiter distributes plates. He can tell there is some serious tension here and hurries quickly away. We are all staring at our food. Only Ryan, who could probably eat during a funeral, digs right in.

M is still crying a little.

I can't stand this. I have to know now, one way or another. I look at M's mom and ask, "So are you saying no? No for sure?"

"I am not saying no, Ariel. I am saying I have a lot of concerns—for Mattie, for your family and what an extra kid for eight months might mean for you all."

My mom chimes in. "We are happy to have her, honestly, but we know you have a lot to weigh and factor in. We respect the decision you make, for you and your daughter, whatever it might be." My mom is such a politician.

And just like that I feel M's mom start to cave in. I don't think she expected my parents to be so positive. Frankly, I didn't know they were going to be like that myself. I now see that they would not tell me their master plan, because they know I would have told M, and she would have pressured her mother by saying my parents were already all for it. No, this is all a setup, I see that clearly now. But I don't mean to complain— how cool is it that my parents want M to come live with us? Way, way, way cool.

We start to eat and the conversation turns less intense. Everyone speaks in hypotheticals, careful to acknowledge that no final decision has been made. Every sentence starts with something like, "If Mattie *were* to stay, how often could she visit?" Or, "For the sake of argument, let's *pretend* she did live with you until June, I would insist on paying you to compensate her food and all that . . ."

Finally, we are done and everything feels less awkward. Ryan wants to order dessert, but no one else does. To get him to stop whining, I tell him I'll make his favorite peanut butter pie tonight, which makes him happy.

My dad insists on paying the bill, and we file out into the sunny afternoon. M's mom says she'll be in touch soon, that she needs to talk to M's dad some more. She thanks my parents for their "generosity" and "warmth." M asks if she can ride the ferry home with us and help me make (and eat) the pie. My parents say that would be fine. The pie has to freeze a long time, so she'll probably stay the night. For some reason that feels critical right now, even though she's stayed over many times.

M's mom shrugs and agrees to the overnight. She says good-bye to us all and hurries up the sidewalk, alone, toward the massive parking structure across from the movie theater. She walks with her head down and her arms crossed, her hands grasping opposite elbows, all folded-in on herself. M stares at her mother's back for a second, and what I think is a look of sadness, or maybe even anger—the two can look alike sometimes—crosses her face for just a moment. Then the ferry horn is calling us and we hurry toward the waiting boat.

Ryan's Peanut Butter Pie
with Reese's Crumbles

1 premade chocolate pie crust (in the baking aisle, or
     make your own using crushed Oreo cookies, about
     15, with 3 T. melted butter mixed together and
     packed into a pie pan)

1 ½ C. milk

⅓ C. sugar

1 t. vanilla

¾ C. chunky peanut butter (works with creamy too, but
     the texture is not as good)

½ package cream cheese (4 oz.)

1 T. lemon juice

1 tub cool whip (NOT frozen)

12 miniature Reese's peanut butter candy cups, crumbled
     up (or you can use more Oreos, crumbled up)

*Cook milk, sugar, and vanilla in a saucepan over medium
heat until the sugar is dissolved (do not boil). Remove the milk
from the heat and stir in the peanut butter until it's totally
melted. Let it cool a little bit, and use the time to chop up the
Reese's candy and make a level surface in the freezer for the
pie. Put the cream cheese on a plate or in a bowl that can go
in the microwave and soften it by cooking it 10 to 15 seconds.
Using a stand mixer or an electric hand mixer, whip the
cream cheese in a large bowl until it's fluffy, whip in the lemon
juice, then whip in the milk/peanut butter mixture until it's
all well-blended. Fold in the Cool Whip, mixing just enough to*

get it incorporated, no more. Pour the filling into the pie crust. Sprinkle the Reese's crumbles over the filling. Use the plastic insert that covered the pie crust when you bought it upside-down (like a dome) to cover the pie. Freeze it until firm, about 6 hours or overnight. Let it sit out a few minutes on the counter before cutting, and run the knife under hot water between each slice.

O-M-G

Back home. Mom, Dad, and Ryan drift back to their typical weekend things. Dad mows the lawn and fiddles in the garage. Mom sits with the newspaper and a stack of magazines, clipping coupons and articles, reading, and humming at the patio table. Ryan is in the basement, presumably lifting weights and imagining his spaghetti-like arms thickening up with the effort. He is such a dreamer. M and I are making the promised pie.

We don't talk much at first. We don't always have to fill the nooks and crannies of being together with words. We can just hang, silent and together. I call instructions ("get the large measuring cup," "rinse this out," "mix that," etc.) and M follows my commands mutely. She knows my kitchen as well as her own, and she knows me better than anyone, so we can do this sort of thing without any formal communication. Plus,

M is always like this . . . she needs time to form her thoughts, and then to translate those into words in her head. Then she has to compose those thoughts into speech. With M, it takes awhile to hear what she has to say. She's like a bread starter that will not be rushed into rising.

Finally, while the mixer is whirring, M starts talking. I figured she would, sooner or later. She washes a bowl and asks, "If you were in my situation, would you leave your mother?"

I consider her question while scraping the bowl with a rubber spatula. The chunky peanut butter makes little funny islands, sinking and popping back up in a beige milk sea. "I don't think we can compare, M. Our mothers are so different."

"I know," she bangs the bowl into the dish strainer and snaps the dishtowel in frustration before continuing. "But you know what I mean. If you had a mom like mine—alone and sort of needful—do you think you would leave her like I am?"

"I think *she* left *you*, M. I mean, not literally, but by making you move like this, well it is a leaving thing, you know?"

M turns the water back on, rinsing a measuring cup. "Yeah, okay. I see what you mean." But M sounds so quiet and sad, and I wonder if she does.

We called Nicki when we first got back, but it kept going to voicemail. When she finally called back, she said her mom had been on the phone with an aunt. I could swear she said her mom took Noah to physical therapy on Saturday afternoons, but I didn't say anything. More and more I am wondering about Nicki. She agreed to come over right away.

She rings the doorbell when she arrives, even though I told her to just come in and find us in the kitchen. She is like a senior citizen in the manners department. M and I try to break her of this severe need to be so correct, so formal, but it is useless. The girl will be a doorbell ringer until the day she dies.

I open the door and say in my old lady voice, "Missy, we don't want anything you might be sellin'."

Nicki giggles a little, and tries to match me by saying, "*Everyone* needs a magazine subscription or an invitation to worship, young lady, so don't be so fast to turn me away!"

I love it when Nicki clowns like this, rare occasion that it is. I grab her by the arm and drag her into the living room. "God, Nicki, that was actually almost funny." It wasn't really *that* funny, but this is Nicki here, and her humor needs to be encouraged.

"Ha ha, Ariel, thanks. Remember, I am the *smart* princess, so stop expecting me to be *witty* too. Don't you need to go comb your hair with a utensil or commune with a seagull?"

I laugh when she says that. Just when Nicki seems chronically serious and quiet, she pipes up with something like this. I still think she is hiding something, but I see her *genuineness* and I think I must be wrong.

Back in the kitchen, M has finished washing the dishes that won't go in the dishwasher. I stop the mixer and take the bowl off the stand, then pour the creamy filling into the waiting crust. Nicki watches, seating herself on her usual barstool in the corner spot.

"What did you guys make?" Nicki asks, nodding to the pile of dishes dripping in the strainer and the pie that is waiting to find a home in the freezer.

"Peanut butter pie. Ryan's favorite," I tell her.

Nick wrinkles her nose in disgust; she hates peanuts, peanut butter, and presumably, peanut butter pie.

"I'm making your favorite fish tacos tonight though. Wanna stay?"

"I can't. My Grammy Clare is here this weekend, and we're going out with her."

M says, before I have even asked, "And I need to get home and talk to my mom."

"The tacos don't keep well, so I can't bring you any leftovers," I warn them. I had hoped M would spend the night. "Remember when I made them last summer after we went to the Exploratorium in San Francisco? You guys both stuffed yourselves and declared me a mermaid goddess for their deliciousness!" I want them to stay. Food is something most people can be bribed with.

"Sorry, Air, just can't," Nicki is obviously a no-sale.

"Soon, maybe, if this happens, I'll never miss your meals, Air," M smiles and rubs her belly. "I'll probably gain a hundred pounds living here."

Nicki giggles. "So it seems like it's going to happen for real, huh?"

"I think so, yeah. I mean, it's up to M's mom," I wedge the pie into the freezer on top of a frozen pizza before continuing, "though just before you got here, Nicki, M was going into a guilt thing. You know, worried about her mother being alone up there."

Nicki looks at M with a sympathetic face. "Oh, yeah, I can see that. I would worry too. She'll feel alone up there and in a new city."

I cut her off quickly. M does not need to be encouraged with the guilt; she's wavering on this as it is. "But, Nicki, *think* about it. Her mom will really want what makes M happiest, right, and it *is* for the best that the poor girl gets to finish the school year here"—M plays a little finger violin for herself when I say this—"where her friends are, where everything she knows is! Plus it's not for that long anyway. We're just talking eight months." I am talking to Nicki but I realize my words are aimed at M.

And then as I'm talking I think of the earthquake. We're all standing about where we were when it struck, but it seems to have been forgotten by everyone but me. It set something in motion. Now I feel like I am trying to prove something or win some argument right now with M even though we are on the same side. It never used to be like that.

I shake my head, push the earthquake theory away from my mind, and say, "I am right, aren't I?"

M raises her eyebrows at me in passive agreement.

Nicki nods. "That's all probably true, Air. I just mean I can see how it would be weird for M too."

M is listening to us talk about her, but not jumping in. I can tell she's really thinking it through now that it seems so possible. She wanders over to the window and stares out. There is uncomfortable silence.

The phone rings and we all jump. I grab it before Ryan can, just to annoy him. He is forever getting it first, hoping some girl is calling.

"Casa de Solomon," I answer as I always do.

"Hello, Ariel. May I speak with Mattie please?" She doesn't bother telling me who it is, and of course I know.

"Um, sure. Hold on." I hold out the phone to M. "It's your mom."

M looks worried for a second, but takes the phone and says, "Mom?" There's about twenty seconds of silence and M is looking at the floor. I can't tell anything from her face. Finally she says, "Wow, okay. Um. Well, wow . . . ," another fifteen seconds of her listening, and she nods her head. "Okay, love you too, bye."

She hangs up. She looks stunned. "My mom said I can do it. Live here. She talked to my dad. You were right, Ariel, she was talking all about how she just wanted me to be happy."

I grab M around the waist and whoop as I swing her around. "OH MY GOD, OH MY GOD," I yell, "this is AWESOME!"

Nicki is clapping her hands and laughing at me as I screech around the kitchen. M looks shocked.

My mom comes in to see what I am yelling about, and we tell her, and she hugs M, who is smiling now, but still looks shaky. I think it's probably excitement.

We head to my room to talk this out. I can't believe my best friend is going to live with me—it is so stupendously thrilling. I know M will love-love-love this year, here, with me, with my family.

As I close the door to my room, about to launch into how we can redesign my room, M bursts into tears.

Mermaid Goddess
Fish Tacos

1 ½ lbs. fresh (or frozen and thawed) boneless white fish
(fresh halibut is the best, but any mild white fish
works)

3 limes (or 3 T. bottled lime juice if you don't have fresh
limes)

salt and pepper

2 avocados, chopped

1 small bag shredded red cabbage

½ C. chopped cilantro (use parsley in a pinch)

1 C. sour cream

1 T. honey

½ t. cumin

salsa

hot sauce

corn tortillas

*The fish cooks very fast, so get everything else ready first. While
you are doing this, let the fish marinate about 15 minutes. Put
the fish in a pan and squeeze two limes (2 T. lime juice) over
it, and sprinkle with salt and pepper. Use a large platter or
cutting board: mound the cabbage on one side, the avocados
on the other side, and leave the middle open for the fish. Mix
the cumin plus 1 T. lime juice and the honey into the sour
cream.*

*Heat a no-stick frying pan over medium-high heat, spray
with cooking spray and cook fish quickly, turning once, about*

3 minutes. Put it on the middle of your platter and use a fork to break it into big pieces. Sprinkle the cilantro over the fish and mix them together a little. Have salsa, hot sauce, sour cream topping, and corn tortillas laid out around the platter. Serve family style; everyone builds their own.

Nicki's Proposal

It has been exactly one week since M moved in and it is supremely cool just like I knew it would be. On her mom's moving day, the movers brought over her bit of furniture (twin bed, white dresser, and a night stand with a drawer that is stuck shut), plus two cardboard boxes holding all M's personal stuff. We immediately arranged our beds into an "L" shape, so that our heads are super-close and we can whisper really quietly and still hear each other, without being heard by anyone who might be walking by the bedroom door.

The day her mom left was uncomfortable. They stood in the corner of their sad, brownish lawn next to the SOLD sign with their backs turned, talking. I could see M gesturing with her hands a lot, but I don't know what they were saying. When they turned back, M's mom was crying hard, silently. She waved half-heartedly to me and my dad, who were there to see her off and take M home with us after she left. She got into her car and was gone. M watched, her arms folded, her eyes dry.

The first days right after that were a tiny bit tense. I didn't realize how our family has all these routines and unspoken codes of understanding. I guess most families probably do, but I never thought about it. For example, when someone in our family says something smart-alecky and picky we call it "Uncle Johning." My Uncle John is known for always pointing out anytime someone accidentally mispronounces a word or trips up in any way.

The first night of M's stay, at dinner, my mom said (accidentally), "Can you pees plass the butter."

Our whole family instantly corrected her with a simultaneous, "PLEASE pass."

Mom rolled her eyes and said, "Thanks a lot, Uncle Johns," and we all laughed. Except M, of course, who had no idea what was funny or what we were even talking about. Then we tried to explain the whole history of the Uncle John thing, but it didn't seem that funny when we tried to explain. It's stuff like that, so ingrained into the fabric of our family—invisible to us, but a mystery to M.

I want M to be happy and comfortable here, so every time some little Solomon family quirk pops up, it makes me worry that she feels out of place here. I try to explain these things when they come up, but it makes me feel a little annoyed that I have to spell it out.

That aside, having M here all the time is awesome. She uses the flat iron on the back of my hair before school (I can never reach and get it to look right), and we share clothes and jewelry, of course. I am looking better for it too. But the best thing is that the "Solomon Family Game Night" has been single-handedly revived by M.

Our family started a weekly game night years ago, but honestly we all got kind of bored with it. My mom always kicked everyone's butts at Scrabble, and my brother never wanted to play anything but Clue, which we all got sick of. My dad would watch sports or news over our shoulders during the games, which was kind of insulting. By the time M moved in, game night had trickled down to a few times a month with only two or three of us usually playing.

M's first night with our family, I suggested we revive the game night and have everyone participate (to make M feel more part of our family). We all sat down to a game of Life, and M was good. The girl can *play*. My dad ignored the TV for once, and at one point Ryan was actually off his seat, arguing good-naturedly that M could not collect her professional ball player salary. It was fun. We have been playing games almost every week since then—M actually beat my mom at Scrabble, and we have gotten to the end of a Monopoly game (who ever does that?). We even bought two new games from the Game Preserve in town (Apples to Apples and Scattergories).

Sometimes M gets really competitive when we play, and I'm surprised that I never saw this side of her before. And it kind of annoys me the way my parents will drop everything to play when M suggests it (I have spent years begging for more game nights, and couldn't usually manage to get my dad away from ESPN), but that's probably petty of me. Mostly it feels like she's done something nice for our family. We're all hanging out together more, and during the games it's like M is a Solomon too. I wish she could live with us forever.

Today is Saturday, and in honor of M's one month anniversary with us, I am making her personal favorite: "Crazy-Good Sausage Lasagna." She actually named it that. It's a recipe I worked really hard on for a turkey sausage cooking contest last fall. It got me an honorable mention and a $25.00 gift certificate for Jennie-O turkey products. Perhaps not a glamorous prize, but it *is* a resume-builder to have the honorable mention, which was printed with my name in *Family Circle.* M still argues that the judges must have had faulty taste buds or just be crazy or stupid because my recipe should have won.

I am making the sauce now, and the kitchen is very warm and smells like anise. The black licorice smell is homey. M is sitting on the floor in the corner of the kitchen, her back against the wall, painting her toenails a vile blue color called "bruise." The white ceramic flour canister that got cracked in the earthquake is above her head, and it makes me shiver, remembering the loud crack of it hitting the ground.

"I need to call my mom sometime today," she says, using her thumb to wipe blue polish from the cuticle of her big toe. She has a prepaid calling card and is supposed to call twice a week, and also call her dad on the weekends, but I don't think she has been. I know my mom reminds her to, but never pushes it. M doesn't talk about her conversations—or lack of—much at all.

"Okay. I was going to catch a new episode of *Bizarre Foods* at three, so wanna call her then?"

"Okay, that'll work." M hates *Bizarre Foods*. It's this show about a guy who travels the world finding the strangest, most bizarre foods, and eating them. The guy will eat any sort of insect, internal organ, etc. I love seeing the incredible variety of foods around the world. M, on the other hand, is squeamish and says watching Andrew (the show's host) eat yak testicles or fried beetles or beating frog hearts (seriously) makes her want to barf. She thinks he's mentally ill. Needless to say, she does her own thing when it's on.

Sometimes Nicki watches it with me, also strangely fascinated. One time she told me it had been something she watched with "someone special," and of course

I had immediately thought of a boyfriend, but she just blushed and rolled her eyes and said it was her cousin. I remember that now and again whenever I have a sense that we are *missing* something with Nicki. I talked about it once to M, but she didn't think Nicki would hide anything from us. She's probably right.

I turn back to M. "After that do you think you might want to watch an episode of *The Sopranos*?"

"Definitely." M caps the bottle of polish and wiggles her toes around, trying to speed the drying. "Do you think Carmela is going to dump Tony soon?"

"She should," I answer.

"I almost blew it and said something about it to my mom last night," M tells me, "but I caught myself."

Okay, here's a confession: M is not supposed to be watching *The Sopranos*. I can't deny that it is chock-full of violence and sex and scandal, because it is. And I am talking about the versions they are rerunning on cable, not even the original, full episodes. Those are still off-limits (my mom said they are too violent even for her to stomach).

It all started last summer. My parents had been TiVoing the series for several months, and they would always talk about the characters or some episode; it was obvious they thought it was a great show and I really wanted to watch it too. They wouldn't let me, which, I guess, for my age, was understandable. I finally broke them down a couple of months ago.

They had let me see *Goodfellas* (I had to beg), which is not exactly a Disney movie, if you know what I mean. After it ended, my mom said she regretted letting me see it, that she felt like it was just way too hardcore. There is a ton of violence in it, not to mention the "f word" being flung around, drugs, and just bad people doing bad stuff. But it is a spectacular story. It is also, to me, *so* unreal. I told my parents about how I felt. We had this big conversation about it all. I told them how I would never act different (like start cussing or something) or even feel different based on seeing some totally fictional, not-at-all-like-real-life mafia movie. No, I didn't think it "glamorized" violence. I mean, these guys die terrible deaths, which is not exactly an advertisement for wanting to go into the mafia. No, I told them, I wouldn't have nightmares. The five o'clock news, now *that's* the nightmare-maker, with real-life stuff like kids getting kidnapped or global warming and drowning polar bears. *That* scares me—not fake Hollywood blood and words with four letters.

After I saw *Goodfellas,* and by then I had already seen the whole *Godfather* series of movies (TV versions, but still), it was only a matter of time and persistence to get permission to watch *The Sopranos.* I think they actually *got* what I said and decided to trust my "maturity." I will admit that I am a tiny bit uncomfortable with some of the violence in *The Sopranos.* I think

I am supposed to be; it is part of how intense the show is. It is a soap opera basically, but much better and I am totally caught up in it.

M's mom forbids "R" movies, even the cleaned-up television versions, and any cable shows that are at all inappropriate. Obviously, she has no idea that M and I are watching *The Sopranos,* and we plan to keep it that way. Of course, my parents don't know how strict M's mom is about this particular thing. I figure that since M lives here now my parent's rules get applied, even if we aren't being exactly aboveboard about it. M was unenthusiastic about the series at first. She said she didn't get my mafia obsession, and couldn't we watch reruns of *Gilmore Girls* instead? I hate that show, and I asked M to just try a couple of episodes of *The Sopranos.* And she got hooked just like I knew she would. Now she's the one who bugs *me* to wedge in more episodes whenever we can.

I am just finishing up assembling the lasagna when Nicki calls. Her parents want to go shopping for a new high chair for Noah, her baby brother, and she doesn't want to get dragged along on a boring errand. Of course I invite her over.

M has disappeared into our room to call her mom, and I am just turning on *Bizarre Foods* when Nicki shows up (she knocks, of course).

"Hey, Nick, you're just in time," I tell her, pointing to the TV where Andrew Zimmern is trotting around

some far eastern food market examining various skew-
ered grubs.

"Where's M?"

"Phone. In my, I mean our room."

"Oh. She hates this show anyway."

"Exactly." I settle into my favorite, battered recliner.

"Ariel?"

"Huh?" I wait, a little irritated that she's talking over
the show. Andrew is deciding between a tasty skewer
of locusts and some sort of organ meat jerky.

"Ms. Oliver called me this morning, at my house."
Ms. Oliver teaches social studies and is Nicki's homeroom teacher.

I turn to her now with my full attention and ask,
"Really? Why?"

"Remember how hard I worked on yearbook last
year?"

"Yeah . . ."

Nicki continues in a rush, "Well, hardly any kids
signed up for yearbook staff this year. The girls I
worked with last year all graduated. It requires two
afternoons a week, at least toward the end, so the kids
that play sports or whatever can't do it. Ms. Oliver
wanted to know if I could get two other kids to commit
to it fully. She would want me to show them that software program, Lifetouch? It's really fun, you can cut
and paste pictures and symbols and stuff . . ."

I interrupt her, turning down the TV volume before

I say, "And you thought M and I would be the perfect 'other two,' right?"

Nicki twirls a section of her long hair, snaking the slick black coil through her fingers in practiced, complicated patterns. "Well, I just think you guys would really like it. M loves photography already, plus she's a computer whiz. And you are so creative with design; I mean look what you can do with a pastry. And you're so outgoing, you could talk to kids, get material. What better thing than three best friends, two who even live together, being the yearbook team?"

I consider. Sounds interesting.

"She needs us to let her know by Monday. She has to get the school board to approve the costs at some meeting and she doesn't want to move forward unless she's positive that a team of students—us—is going to see it through."

"It's a lot of time though." I think it sounds fun, but I don't know about being so *relied* on.

Nicki's hair twirling goes into high gear. The hair is whipping through her fingers now, making a sound like slick fabric. "But it's fun! And if we don't, there probably won't even *be* a yearbook at all. Our last year in junior high, M's last year here at all." She looks up with those huge sad eyes. "Air, I need to keep busy. Don't try to analyze me for that, I just do. This will help."

Hmm. Interesting. I start to analyze it.

M comes in just then. There is a whitish ring around

the outside of her lips as though she's been pursing them a long time. "What's up?"

We tell her about yearbook.

She plops down on the floor next to Nicki's feet. M is a floor-sitter most of the time, I have noticed.

"What would happen if I wasn't here through the end of the year though?" she asks Nicki.

"Mattie-M-Matilda, of course you will be!" What is she saying? Why wouldn't she be?

She looks up at me, and I can feel Nicki watching us. "I mean, I will be, but you know, just in case something happens or whatever."

"Like what?" I ask.

She just shrugs.

"I think we should do it!" I stand up, facing Nicki.

I can see it now, the three of us laying out pages and having yearbook-themed sleepovers. I'll make lots of finger foods to keep us going. We will drink coffee from Starbucks, working into the night to make our deadlines. I imagine us reviewing digital pictures of our classmates and laughing over the shots where some popular girl looks bad or some dork looks cute. I will get to screen my own pictures, and only allow shots that minimize chest and maximize height. I can visualize our three names in the front of the book under some important, bolded caption like "STAFF." Most importantly, doing this will pull the three of us together like a drawstring. Like our magic book did last summer. M will forget to worry about her mom, and Nicki will not sneak around talking for hours on the phone and lying about it.

Nicki smiles at me, and turns to M, waiting.

"Okay." M sounds less excited than me—the only way I can think to describe her slumped shoulders and tone is . . . flat. She is being a little odd. Maybe her mother upset her when they spoke.

Anyway, I am not going to worry about it because I'll talk her into loving this. Once she thinks about it, how much influence we can have at school, how much time the three of us will spend together, she'll come around.

Crazy-Good
Sausage Lasagna

1 t. olive oil

1 lb. Italian turkey sausage (if it's link, squeeze the sausage
   out of the casings before cooking)

1 C. diced onion

3 garlic cloves, minced, or 1 t. crushed garlic from a jar

¼ C. diced celery

¼ C. diced carrot

1 C. white cooking wine

1 C. milk

1 lg. can chopped Italian tomatoes

1 t. ground nutmeg

pinch of cayenne pepper

2 cups shredded mozzarella cheese

1 cup grated parmesan cheese

boxed, no-cook lasagna noodles

1 small can tomato paste

butter

*Heat olive oil over medium heat. Add sausage; crumble it
up with a wooden spoon as it cooks. When it is well cooked
and crumbly, drain off the fat by dumping the meat into a
colander or strainer. Return it to the pan and add the onion,
garlic, carrot, and celery. Cook five minutes, stirring often.
Add cooking wine and cook until it is evaporated and mixture
is almost dry again. Turn down the heat a bit and add milk,
again cooking and stirring until the milk is evaporated. Add*

tomatoes and nutmeg, reduce heat to low, and simmer about one hour, or until the sauce is thick and there's very little liquid left. Set sauce aside. Mix the water and tomato paste until smooth, in a separate bowl. Get ready to layer! In a 13x9" pan, spread the tomato paste mixture on the bottom, lay a single layer of lasagna noodles over this, put a third of the mozzarella cheese on the noodles, spoon a third of the tomato sauce over this, then sprinkle it with parmesan cheese. Continue to layer in this order until you run out of ingredients; be sure to end with parmesan cheese. Dot with butter all over, using about a tablespoon. Bake 45 minutes at 400°, or until golden and bubbly. Cool 10 minutes before cutting.

M is for Meadow?

I love Mondays at my house. On Mondays Island
Sweets is closed, and my dad stays home all day. It is
the one night he cooks dinner, and he always barbe-
cues. Even in the rain, he'll wheel the grill under the
overhang in our backyard and forge ahead. And Dad
is not stuck in the usual barbecue mindset which involves only hamburgers, hot dogs, steaks, and chicken.
Oh no. He will make all sorts of stuff using his beloved
grill; this year alone we have had beef stroganoff, corn-
bread, potato soup, and cheese soufflés off the grill. In
fact, I first got interested in cooking when I was really
little by helping him try out barbecue recipes. Over
the years, we became a team. Dad would figure out
what main course to grill, and then ask me to make
some side dish to accompany it.

We meet with Ms. Oliver on Mondays for yearbook,

so M and I don't get home until almost 5:00. We throw our backpacks and jackets in a pile near the front door, and head to the kitchen, starving.

My dad's busy at the cutting board. There are piles of bell peppers in red, orange, yellow, and green piled next to him. He turns as we come in, "Hi, girls, how was yearbook?"

I kiss Dad's cheek and grab a red pepper spear, crunching down with satisfaction, as I tell him how fun this yearbook project is going to be. I offer a pepper to M, but she wrinkles her nose and shakes her head. I should have remembered.

"I hate bell peppers," she says, then instantly realizes this is not exactly a tactful comment, given the fact my dad is obviously getting ready to cook lots of bell peppers. She tries to backpedal, "I mean, they aren't my favorite, but I can eat them . . ."

My dad laughs and gives her shoulder a little pat. "Don't worry about it, Mattie. I was going to make steak and pepper skewers, but I can make you a steak-only version, and you can grab some salad left from last night. Besides, I am going to kick your behind on that Sorry! board tonight." Why's he being so nice when M has been rude?

He turns back to the chopping board and starts mincing garlic for his basting sauce. The kebobs are such a traditional barbecue food, not at all like his usual creative efforts—I realize he must have been conservative on account of M. And still it backfired. I feel bad for him, and a small flare of irritation at her for being insensitive and picky blooms in my head for an instant. I squelch it.

M thanks Dad. We grab a couple of green apples from the fruit bowl, and I forage in the fridge for a hunk of sharp cheddar to accompany the tart fruit. There is no better snack.

"I have a script for my next cable spot," my dad tells us. I pop a fat apple wedge and sliver of cheese into my mouth and roll my eyes at M.

She swallows her own mouthful of crunchy apple and cheese before asking, "Is it another *Godfather* thing?"

"Just what I need," I say jokingly. "More material for kids at school to roll their at eyes at me."

"Well, darling daughter," Dad says, not without his own touch of sarcasm, "you'll be happy to hear that the mafia theme continues. But, no, not *The Godfather*. It's a *Sopranos* spoof this time."

M looks instantly intrigued. "Really?"

"Uh-huh." Dad's brow furrows for a moment as he says, "Have you seen *The Sopranos*, Mattie?"

Like I said, we haven't exactly been public about watching the episodes. I cut in quickly, before M blows it with a confession. "What's the new ad's plot, Dad? What's it based on? Tell us about it."

Dad turns back to the cutting board, instantly falling

into my distraction trap. He loves to talk about his ads, about how they're so funny and clever. M cuts her eyes at me and gives me a silent, O-lipped "woo" that says "that was close."

Dad tells us about the script. He will play Tony (and given his Santa-like stomach, this is actually a role he will resemble without much effort). Mrs. Kaiser, the lady who does his books at the store, will play Carmela, Tony's wife. Mrs. Kaiser looks like she's had a hard life—she smokes and it looks like she uses a trowel to put on her make-up, so she'll make a good mafia wife.

He tells us about the script. Basically, Carmela will discover a locked, suspicious-looking case of what she imagines is contraband. Like guns or drugs or something. She'll use actual dialogue from an episode to go off on Tony for bringing his dangerous stuff into the house with the kids. Dad says Mrs. Kaiser has already practiced a lot, trying to sound just like Edie Falco, the actress who plays Carmela. Then Meadow, Tony and Carmela's daughter, will come in. She'll demand to know what's going on, and Tony (Dad) will dramatically throw open the chest to reveal piles of hand-crafted chocolates. They will all gasp and look at Tony in horror as the picture fades out and the screen says, "Island Sweets. So Good They Should Be Illegal."

Dad finishes his description. I am already picturing how cheesy this is going to be. I say nothing, even though he half turns to me as he stops talking, waiting for a response.

"I want to be Meadow!" M blurts out.

Dad turns back to face M, "What?"

"I want to be in your commercial and play Meadow!" M sounds all excited. I am still speechless.

"But you haven't seen *The Sopranos* . . ." Dad is thinking about it, rubbing his chin reflectively. He assumes M's lack of response about seeing *The Sopranos* when it came up a little while ago means she hasn't, and neither of us rushes to fill him in on reality.

"M, come on, you don't want to do this. I mean, it'll be totally dorky."

"I don't think so," she says to me, "I think it'll be fun. You're always saying I need to be more outgoing, Air."

"I think we could make it work," Dad says. He is warming to the idea, "I don't have anyone to be Meadow yet—maybe you could watch just a couple of episodes that aren't too . . . harsh. Just to get down how Meadow talks. And we could get you a long, dark wig." He is getting all fired-up now. Great.

"Ariel watches *The Sopranos*, Mr. Solomon. I think I can handle it too," M tells him. "Especially since it would be like research, and I know my mom would understand."

Dad is full-on smiling now, loving the idea of M in his dumb TV spot. "Well, Mattie, you need to ask her before anything else, okay? But if she's alright with it, I think you'd be a great Meadow!"

"Thanks! I'll call her right now." M practically runs out of the kitchen.

I feel an achy pulse in my temples, and my neck is knotted as I watch her practically skip out. I notice that someone—probably my mother—has cut some marigolds from our backyard and put them in an ugly decoupage vase I made in second grade. The flowers are so ridiculously bright they look like Caltrans workers. I grab them, bending the stems in half, and toss them in the trash.

"Why'd you do that, Air?" Dad stares at me curiously.

"They're ugly, Dad. Blinding. And that vase . . ." I roll my eyes.

Dad just shrugs and turns back to his work, humming a tuneless song.

I don't know exactly why it is hitting me like this, why I am compelled to murder flowers and glower at my father's bald spot. I mean, Dad has asked me a gazillion times to be in his ads, and I've always said no. They are so corny. He stopped asking after awhile. Now M is into it, and he's thrilled, and why is it all so, so, I don't know, irritating? Am I jealous? Worried about her looking dumb? Unsettled because she's not the shy, take-no-risks girl I have known since preschool?

Dad interrupts my thoughts, "I need something to

go with the skewers, Snarfblatt. Maybe that black bean pot you make, that goes right on the grill? You know, with the lime juice?"

I nod at him, of course I know—I have made it lots of times to accompany his barbecue. I am not trying to mask that I am upset, but he doesn't seem to notice. He turns back to his vegetable piles and starts humming.

I chop the tomatoes savagely, making loud, angry, satisfying thwacks. M comes back into the kitchen. "My mom says she trusts you, and that it's cool, I can see *The Sopranos*, to watch how Meadow acts, and be in your commercial!"

"Okay, Mattie. Great!" Dad winks at her.

M and Dad babble on about it. I finally can't stand it anymore. I slam down my chef's knife, making the can of beans next to me jump and skitter. I can feel both of them are startled, suddenly quiet, watching me as I stalk out.

I sit on my bed until I realize that I am being a drama queen. I go back out and give them a small smile. We end up having a really nice dinner, and afterward my dad really does trounce M on the Sorry! board.

Black Beans
on the Barbecue

3 whole scallions (also called spring onions or green
    onions)
1 tomato, chopped
2 T. fresh cilantro (or 1 t. dried)
1 t. salt
½ t. pepper
¼ t. cumin
3 T. lime juice
2 cans black beans (30 to 36 oz. total), do not drain

*Put all the ingredients in a cast iron pot and mix to combine.
Place on hot barbecue, stir occasionally. Heat until "bean
juice" is syrupy and the mixture is bubbling and hot. Can be
made on the stove top too, of course.*

Earthquake Way-Aftershock

It's been a whole week since M decided to do dad's commercial. I have told her I think it is a mistake, but she is really into it and doesn't care if it does get her teased. At one point she did tell me she would drop out of it if I was going to stay mad. I guess I had been sulking. I admit it. For example, one day after school I was toasting pumpkin seeds for a snack because Ryan's cute friend, Troy, was coming over to our house after practice. I had made this snack once when he was here before, and he said they were strangely addictive, so I was going to impress him again with the lovely little roasted seeds. M had asked me what I was making and I said "pepitas" and turned away. They *are*, technically, called pepitas, but I knew M wouldn't know this, and I could have just said pumpkin seeds. I could have even told her I was making them because Troy had said he liked them. But I didn't. I know it's not very nice, but I can't seem to stop doing this kind of little stuff.

At the same time, she is still good ol' M—the friend I have had forever who knows everything about me. We have really great talks after lights-out, and my grades are better with her around to help me. Family game nights are terrific, and she fits right in with all the competition and teasing. I am confused, and I can't figure it out.

Maybe we should have had it out then, the pumpkin seed day, but we didn't. I hoped she would decide to drop the commercial anyway and go back to being how she usually is. She didn't. I know I should just be cool with it. And I have been struggling not be so bothered about it, and also just trying to figure out why this thing is making me so irritated at M. Because the truth is that this reaction I am having is bothering me about *me*. I tried to call Nicki to talk it out, but her mom said she was out.

But it must also be stated that M and her "acting" obsession are inescapable in my house—I can't get away from it. My dad is constantly scheming with her, and has even written a second commercial already, one that is more Meadow-centered. They're going to shoot both of them in a couple of weeks. My mom is going to take M shopping to buy her brown contacts because Meadow has brown eyes. Ryan told her he would "run lines" with her anytime (as if they are making a

Hollywood blockbuster or something). These days, in the evenings, all M wants to do is watch *The Sopranos*.

Every time I have to hear something about M's Meadow role it makes me feel like I have a little pebble in my shoe. It's dull and small but just drives me crazy. That tiny pebble is starting to feel huge.

Seeing M take notes on Meadow's mannerisms, or how she dresses, while we're watching *The Sopranos* has become that pebble. Hearing my dad and her go over every tiny, unimportant detail of their scripts, and listening to her ask Ryan which wig he likes as she looks for a "Meadowhead" online (my dad's new, jokey little nickname for M) . . . it's all pebble-in-the-shoe stuff. She has like three lines and about one minute of actual screen time. And that's for both ads! And anyway, the spots will only show on our dumb little local cable channel. My family is acting like M is going on Broadway. M and I don't talk about any of it. Come to think of it, we haven't been talking about much of anything at all lately.

— —

We are having our second yearbook meeting today, since it's Monday again, with Ms. Oliver. We get to use the computer lab, so we can all work at the same time, on a separate computer. Nicki is showing us how to use Lifetouch, the software for designing the pages.

I am using a program that makes pictures into shapes

that fit together like puzzle pieces. I can't get one of the corners to line up right, so I interrupt Nicki, who is checking off names on a list of kids in the drama club.

"Nick, can you help me?"

She makes a check on her list, marking her place, and leans over my screen.

"Are you going for an abstract background here, or more of a rectangular puzzle frame?" She mouses over a few pieces, rearranging them into different patterns on my screen.

"I want it to be like a *Where's Waldo?* frame, you know, so kids have to look close to find themselves. I want it to be like a real puzzle."

"Uh-huh. Good idea, Ariel, you're a natural at this! You just have to uncheck the autoformatting box, and you can drag and drop the pieces individually."

I do what she says, and start to arrange the pieces in a complicated pattern, morphing their sizes and overlapping the edges. It looks very cool. Who knew it could be this fun.

Nicki goes back to her list, and I sink into my picture puzzle project, sighing contentedly. Besides these sessions on the computer, we also have to go "out in the field" as yearbook staff, but I think I can handle that too.

Ms. Oliver has given each of us a digital camera (from the photo lab) to use for the year, and we will take them everywhere, getting candid pictures of kids at lunch and in the halls, pictures of assemblies, sports practices, and that kind of thing. Nicki, for all her shyness, is a tiger about getting "the shot." Most people know she's "the yearbook girl" and will pose for her, or at the least just ignore her if she's pointing her camera in their face. She's already gotten at least fifty pictures, and I have downloaded another two dozen.

I crop a funny picture of our PE teacher sticking out his tongue while I mentally tally up the events I need to take pictures of this week. There is a basketball game Friday I may go to, and I know Nicki plans to stop by the parent club meeting to get pictures of the worker-bee moms. That leaves no one covering the football scrimmage.

"M," I tilt back in my chair so I can see her, typing away on Nicki's other side, "can you go to the football scrimmage on Friday? Nick and I are already going to be taking pictures for basketball and . . ."

M doesn't look up from her computer, where she slumps in her chair. She types using heavy, slow strokes as she interrupts me. "I don't think so, no."

Nicki's shoulders tense a little. I sit back, straightening up, sighing, not replying, and start to work on my puzzle pieces again. Suddenly the whir of our computers seems very loud.

Nicki smacks her pen down, claps her hands together, and says, "Well, *I* am ready for a break from this list," she taps her paper and scrunches up her forehead. "What do you say we tackle that plan now?"

Ms. Oliver is having us develop a "project plan" that will map out how we will divide everything up and get it done by May, when the yearbook draft will have to be finished.

Nicki wants us each to be responsible for creating a set number of pages. "I will take on the most, of course," she tells us, "and you guys can pick which ones you want. Like, Air, you would obviously want to do the Home Ec. page and probably the volleyball, since you used to play. M, you could do drama, maybe?"

M has obviously been zoning out, not listening. She startles back to earth, and looks at Nicki, "What?"

Nicki sighs, a bit irritated, which is unusual for her. "I am asking you which pages you want to do. We are going to assign them and keep track on this project plan form Ms. Oliver gave us." Near the end of her sentence Nicki's voice drops back into its normal, soft-sounding range. She can't stay annoyed with anyone for more than ten seconds.

"Just, you know, whatever you think, Nicki," M says, "you can pick which pages you want me to do."

Nicki considers. "Okay, I'll give you the club pages, like drama, student government, and debate club. That shouldn't be too hard to put together." She begins writing on the form in front of her. "All three of us need to download and review any pictures we've taken every week, during these Monday meetings. That way we can add to our pages a little at a time, see places we might need more pictures."

Ms. Oliver, grading papers at a large desk at the back of the room, chimes in, "And don't forget, Nicki, to figure out the student voting and questionnaire stuff too. You know, the funny interview for graduating eight-graders, and the awards." Ms. Oliver makes little quotation marks with her fingers around the word "awards."

Nicki nods at Ms. Oliver. "Yeah, I have it down already," she taps the paper with the eraser on her pencil, "and I thought Ariel would be good for getting that part taken care of."

She looks at me and flutters her eyelashes. "Please, Air?"

"I guess, but why me?"

"Because you're perfect for it. You aren't shy, you can draw people out for the interviews, and you're funny. You'll think of good awards."

M interrupts, "Could I do that?"

Nicki looks startled. "Would you want to? I mean, you would have to talk to each of the eighth-graders personally. But you could—that is, you can, it's just that I didn't think you would like that sort of thing, M. I just thought Air would be more comfortable . . ."

M turns to Nicki. She looks angry. "Oh, okay. Whatever."

Nicki is instantly remorseful, worried she's hurt M's feelings. "I didn't mean you *can't*, or anything like that, and it's great if you want to. Of course you could handle it! Ariel, don't you think M could handle this? Maybe you guys could do it together!" Poor Nicki, she is always trying to smooth things over, so worried about any tiny hurt, real or imagined. If she thinks she is the cause of an emotional wound, well that tips her over the edge.

Ms. Oliver chimes in, sensing the sudden tension and trying to squash it, "You girls'll work it all out! The interviews and awards sections can happen down the road anyway, so no need to get into the details right now. I have to leave, but you three can stay and work until 5:00 if you like. Or until the custodian boots you out."

Nicki thanks her. After the door shuts behind her, Nicki turns back to M. "Are we okay? Are you mad at me? You should do the interviews, M. Okay?" If Nicki says "okay" one more time in that begging tone *I* will not be *okay*.

M is picking a cuticle, staring intently at the little strip of flesh as it tears. I wince, knowing that's gotta hurt. Without looking up she says, "You're right, Nicki. About me not being suited to playing the outgoing, fun interviewer." She puts her injured finger in her mouth for a second, nursing the tender, raw flesh she has exposed.

Nicki shakes her head so hard her hair actually makes a snapping sound. "No! That isn't what I meant, M! I just figured you wouldn't be comfortable. But it's *great* if you are!"

M goes back to work on the cuticle, picking tiny pieces of skin at its edges, widening the puffed, sore looking circumference of the wound. "No, Nicki, I think you were right. In fact, I think this whole yearbook thing is not for me. I don't think I am going to do it." She looks at me, "You will be perfect to do the interviews and awards stuff, Air. Nick's right." I don't detect any sarcasm. Usually I know M so well, but I have no idea what's going on with her now.

Nicki freaks. "Oh my God, no, M, don't quit! I'm sorry, okay? I need you—we need you. The yearbook needs you!" She has gone from begging to shameless pleading.

M shrugs. "I'm sorry, Nicki, but I never really wanted to do this anyway. And I *am* busy with the commercials. Being Meadow."

I stare at her and can't help letting out a snort. "M, it's two thirty-second spots on local cable. They'll be sandwiched between a rerun of *Little House on the Prairie* and an ad for hemorrhoid cream! And my dad says you only have one or two hours of rehearsal. It's not a big deal . . ."

M slaps her palm down on the desk. "Maybe it *is* a big deal to me. You've been weird about it ever since I decided to be Meadow. I don't get it. You're supposed to be my best friend? I don't know why, Ariel, but you hate that I have this. And it's *all* I have right now. I'm not like you, with your big happy family and your game nights and rock-solid plans to be a chef. I mean, why do you even care? Are you jealous? You never even wanted anything to do with your dad's commercials, and he asked you for years! I don't know what I want to be, or do, and maybe I want to try acting." M literally runs out of breath, she shakes her head at me and I look away.

She turns to Nicki now, "And Nicki, maybe I *want* to interview kids and stuff. Maybe I am not as shy as I was last year. I'm not mad at you, but I just realize this is wrong for me. I am officially not doing yearbook as of right now, okay? Who knows if I'll even be here until the end of the year." She shoots me a look when she says this. "Nope, I am out." She stops speaking abruptly, putting her now shredded finger right in front of her mouth and blowing on it, her lips in a perfectly round little O.

Nicki is starting to cry. "I am so, so, so sorry, M. If you want to do the interviews and awards pages I would *love* it! But please, don't quit yearbook." Nicki is pleading, but it is obvious, looking at M's face, that she is not going to come around.

M turns to me. "Are you sorry too, Ariel?"

I feel like I have done something terrible, but what?

Pointed out the obvious, that the commercials with my dad are a minor thing at most? It's the truth, and I feel a sudden rush of righteous anger that M is acting like I am some mean-spirited person with a perfect life. As if. And she is hurting poor Nicki, who does not deserve this treatment. She has already committed, and now she's just going to quit? I feel like we're in the middle of that earthquake and everything is shifting and scraping against everything else.

I say coolly, "M, I am sorry that you are so worked up, but that's all I can think of to be sorry for."

She stares at me a moment and I feel like we have crossed some horrible invisible line with each other. I know now why I had the sense that that earthquake set something in motion all those months ago. I fully believe in the sixth sense, that all of us have premonitions about our futures if we are willing to be open to recognizing them. During that earthquake I sensed something terrible beginning to slide toward me, from the future. And all the flashbacks over the following weeks—reminders of the earthquake's damage. I have been reminded in all sorts of little moments to prepare for the big aftershock. And here it is: I am losing my oldest, best friend.

Strangely Addictive
Pepitas

1 lb. raw pumpkin seeds (called "pepitas" in Spanish.
    They are sometimes on the nut aisle, or sometimes
    in the ethnic foods section, as they are used a lot in
    Mexican cooking)
1 T. olive oil
2 t. seasoning salt
1 t. garlic powder
¼ t. pepper

Heat a skillet over medium heat, add the pumpkin seeds and drizzle with the oil. Stir and mix the seeds frequently as they cook—they burn easily if left in one spot too long. When they are just starting to turn brown, are fragrant, and are starting to "pop," sprinkle with seasonings. Stir and cook 2 more minutes. Cool the seeds spread out on a cookie sheet (don't leave them in the pan; they'll continue to cook, and burn). When cooled to room temperature, put them in a bowl and watch them disappear.

M Gets "Sick"

I am walking the Bay Farm Island trail alone, watching the sun sink toward the bay. I came here straight from our disastrous yearbook meeting. I pass the place Nicki, M, and I once buried our most cherished objects, hoping to cast a spell of change. I wish we could go back to that time, when magic seemed possible. I start to walk more quickly.

For so many years this trail has been a place of comfort, friendship, discovery, and thinking. It is no wonder I came here now. Because I need to think, that's for sure. I can't go home to my room either, which is normally where I retreat in crisis moments, because it isn't even my space anymore. It's M's too. Things have become horribly tangled up.

As I walk, I remember this childish game I used to play of predicting the future. I would make up little questions for the universe to answer, and say them out loud. I used to say things like, *A plane will fly over my head in the next five minutes if I get to go to the birthday sleepover.* Or, *A bird will sing in the next two minutes if Jason likes me.* I used to feel like the universe already knew everything that would happen, and I could tap into this preset future with my technique. Of course, planes overhead and singing birds, on this trail, are about as common as clouds in the sky, so I'll admit I kind of stacked the deck most of the time.

By the time my age got into the double digits I abandoned my prediction game (it had been boringly successful), and started offering more of a multiple choice sort of format to the cosmos. Actually, M and I developed this method for decision-making together. When something came up that we really couldn't decide about by talking, we would pass the decision on to the universe, usually in whispers as we walked this trail. And we always, always, stuck to the verdict we were handed back.

I remember one time, about two years ago, I really wanted to take a summer class at this cooking college in the City. The age limit was sixteen, and I was twelve at the time. My parents told me to forget it, that the age limit would exclude me, and plus they didn't want me riding BART and walking around San Francisco alone. I thought I might be able to write to the admissions people and convince them to make an exception for me. I had won a couple of recipe contests by then, and I knew I could show them how mature I was in an interview. I desperately wanted to take this class.

M and I had walked the trail that day and talked about it. Finally, M told me she thought I should toss it out for a "universe decision" (that's what we called it). She even offered to do it for me, and I accepted. She had looked up the trail, squinting at a figure in the distance, then chanted, as she squeezed my hand, "If that lady walking the dog up the trail says hello to us and her dog barks, Ariel will apply for the summer class at California Culinary Academy and they will waive the age limit for her, but if the lady ignores us and her dog is quiet, Air will obey her parents and wait until she's older." We had waited anxiously for the lady with the dog to get to us. We walked slowly, casually, without talking again, careful not to influence the outcome by encouraging the woman or the dog in any particular way.

Finally, the woman was just a few feet away, but gazing over the water and not noticing us at all. We had scooted to the side of the trail, waiting to see what would happen as we shuffled by. When the woman was about a foot away, she snapped her gaze from the bay and made eye contact, smiling, and said, "Hello, girls! Enjoying your walk?" *And* her dog barked several throaty, happy barks as they passed. It felt miraculous.

M and I had looked at each other in wonder—we would have settled for a shy "hi" and a growl from the dog and considered *that* the universe's positive response, so such an undeniably obvious answer was just absolutely spine-tingling. It was so certain.

But it had been a disaster. I learned that the universe sometimes made bad choices. I had written a letter to the admissions office. M had helped me work and rework each sentence, trying to make me sound mature and like I was practically a child-chef-prodigy-wonder-girl.

A week later, someone from the Academy had called my parents. Of course, my parents had already told me I couldn't apply, and didn't know I had anyway, so, needless to say, they were not thrilled to get this call. The Academy explained that if they let one underage person in they would have to let in others—that old, tired argument everyone uses about making exceptions. My parents were angry, and I had been grounded for two weeks. I also got my computer taken away, and I wasn't allowed to watch TV. What really hurt was that it was all for nothing anyway because I couldn't get in. I felt like the universe had wronged me, tricked me.

I feel the same way now. My whole life is mixed into M and her life. It was always so purely good with us and now it's so bad. I don't know how we got to that place, and so fast. Walking on this trail, thinking about

the "universe decision" and even the stupid dog yap-
ping in the distance all remind me of her. Of us. I've
always figured the universe would never, ever see fit to
break us apart, but now we are just that. Broken. As I
walk I try to understand what has happened. Why do I
have this hard seed of anger nestled in my chest practically all the time? What do I do now? I can't unravel it
anymore.

My thoughts turn to an easier problem—Nicki.
Something is going on with her. There's her weird
phone calls and the way she lies about them. More
and more she seems frantic to get home, yet at other
times desperate to stay at school and bury herself
in yearbook work. I roll my head from side to side,
trying to unknot my aching neck muscles. It occurs
to me that M and I don't really *know* know Nicki. I
know something is going on with her. But what?

God, things are a mess. I sigh loudly and
dramatically—there's no one close by—and scream out
loud, "What is UP with everyone?" Maybe I should try
scream therapy. I feel somewhat better.

I have to turn around because it is getting dark
soon. It's that time near dusk, just before sunset, that
makes little kids become temporarily insane—mad to
squeeze every drop of playtime from the almost-done
day, knowing dark and dinner and bed are so close.
I remember the feeling; that frantic burst of twilight
energy thrumming in my veins. When we were little,

Ryan and I would spin around in crazy circles on our lawn, falling down and laughing like maniacs in the last light before sunset. Thinking about this makes me wish I were still five years old, when things were simple.

Right now I feel the opposite way. The setting sun gives me a heavy, tired feeling. I turn around and drag myself back down the trail and over the footbridge. Cars have their headlights on, and they flash over me in bright, rippled stripes as I walk. I feel exposed and vulnerable suddenly. But I dread going home, so I don't hurry too much. As it is, I'll probably get a lecture for being out alone. They'll know that the year-book meeting is over because M left over an hour ago. Reluctantly, I quicken my pace.

It is almost all the way dark when I walk into our yard. The house is lit up, as always, and I can hear music coming from the living room. I bang the door shut to announce my arrival. No one yells out or says anything. I drop my stuff and head to the kitchen.

My mom is on the phone. She gives me a little wave and holds up three fingers, mouthing silently, "Off in three." My dad isn't home yet. M and Ryan are no-where to be seen. Celine Dion belts out a sappy song on the oldies station my mom likes. Everything seems overly warm and too loud and bright after the cool dusk outside.

I grab a handful of grapes from a bowl on the counter and perch on a barstool while I wait for my mom to get off the phone. I wonder what M told her, I wonder where M is.

Finally, Mom hangs up. "Hey, Air, how was your meeting?" She asks casually, as she pulls salad stuff out of the fridge. She's not mad, that's obvious. Hmm.

"Uh, fine, Mom."

"That's good." She eyes a cucumber suspiciously, pressing her thumb on it. She makes a face as her thumb sinks in, and throws it away. Obviously she doesn't know anything about the yearbook meeting. M must have somehow covered for me. This is actually worse than getting yelled at . . . if M had at least ratted me out or gotten me in trouble at home, I could feel righteous about being so ticked off at her. As it is, I feel even more frustrated and annoyed. I can't tell if I feel that way about me or about her at this point.

My mom notices something, perhaps an expression I have, as I consider these possibilities, and asks, "Everything okay?"

"Yeah, Mom." I act casual. "Why?"

"No reason, really. You just looked worried for a second. Hope you aren't getting whatever it is that sent M home. She looked awful, but you know that, I'm sure. She said it came over her in the yearbook meeting. She's lying down now."

Okay, so that's the story. M hasn't told Mom about our fight. "Uh, yeah, she wasn't feeling well."

Mom is chopping tomatoes. "She is going to pass on dinner, so let's just let her rest. There is a stomach flu going around," Mom shakes her head and sighs. "Poor M must have it. She looked so pale! She said she would sleep on the couch tonight, so you don't get whatever she has, but I told her I knew you wouldn't want that. *She* should be in bed, in a quiet place. So you can take the couch if you're worried about getting her bug. I guess we'll skip the game tonight."

"Okay, I'll take the couch."

I feel a little flare of victory, justification for the way I have treated M, because she is kicking me out of my own room. And cancelling game night is actually a relief. I don't think we could play a game in front of everyone and not get into it.

I grab the phone to call Nicki. I need to see what side she is on, mine or M's. Her mom answers and says Nicki is at a yearbook meeting, but should be home soon. The "meeting" ended over an hour ago, M was already here, so where is Nicki? My head aches.

Suddenly I need to make something. I can't stand this level of tension, all the deception and half-truth I find myself buried in. I have to be in the kitchen, working, alone. I need to stop thinking about M, about Nicki, about earthquakes and fate. Throwing myself into a cooking project is the only way to get out of my own head. It always has been for me—when I'm working through a recipe I get absorbed by the process and there is no room for anything else. I feel almost desperate to sink into something and forget the mess of my life, at least for a little while.

"Mom, don't you have a PTA meeting tomorrow?" I had seen it, written in Mom's slanty writing, marked on the kitchen wall calendar.

"Yes, hon. Why?"

"Do you want me to make something for it? I have been working on a recipe for a contest sponsored by Dannon. It's a contest for baking with yogurt. Anyway, I want to try an idea I have for a pound cake."

Mom shrugs, "Sure, honey, everyone loves your baked stuff. And so many women in PTA are worried about their diets, so something less sinful will be welcome. But don't you have homework?"

"No, I'll do it later tonight, and I *feel* like making something."

Mom shrugs, covering the salad she has made with plastic wrap, "Okay, you can have the kitchen until your dad gets home. Then I'll need to cook the fish."

"An hour's fine, Mom." I take her arm and push her out, "but I gotta get started now."

Mom smiles at me and ruffles my hair. "Yes, ma'am, I'm leaving!" She turns in the doorway, "Do you want to check in on M, or should I?"

I shrug. I plan to avoid M as long as I can, as long as it is possible to avoid someone who lives in your house. Someone who, in fact, has taken over your room. "Um, can you? I want to get started . . ." I wrap my apron around me snuggly, starting to think about coming up with a good ratio for using yogurt as a butter substitute in a cake. Already everything else is fading as my thoughts turn to the recipe, the ingredients, and the process of making something unique and tasty. The cake is my therapy session.

Mom nods her head and goes down the hall to "my" room. I get out the eggs and yogurt thinking through portions and cooking times, combing my memory for baking recipes I've made before that involve yogurt. I know the M situation will not go away, but at least I can escape from it for a little while.

Lighten-Up Therapy
Pound Cake

3 C. dark brown sugar

8 T. light, unsalted butter

2 eggs

6 egg whites

3 C. sifted flour

½ t. baking soda

1 ½ C. plain, low-fat, or non-fat yogurt

1 T. finely grated lemon zest

2 T. lemon juice

3 T. poppy seeds

Preheat oven to 325°. Soften the butter in the microwave for 10 seconds. Use an electric mixer to combine the butter with the sugar, beating until it's light and fluffy. Add the eggs and egg whites a little at a time, beating well after each addition. Add the yogurt, lemon zest and juice, and poppy seeds, mixing until incorporated. Measure the flour and mix the baking soda into it. Add the dry ingredients to the wet in three parts, mixing after each addition, just until barely mixed in. Don't overmix. Even if the flour is not quite all the way mixed in, stop, and use a big spoon to finish the last bit by hand, using as few strokes as possible. The cake can be cooked in a Bundt (tube) cake pan or in a loaf pan, coated with butter and flour (or a butter/flour baking spray). Bake for 1 ½ hours (Bundt) or 1 hour 50 minutes (loaf pan), or until a toothpick inserted near center comes out clean and the cake is starting to pull away from the edges of the pan. Cool in pan 15 minutes, and then turn onto cooling rack to cool completely.

Living Room Camping

I have just settled onto the couch and made it my temporary spot. I dragged an end table over and arranged my water, alarm clock, flashlight, Kleenex, and the book I am reading in approximately the same way they were on the bed stand in my room. I had to sneak into my own room to get most of this stuff. I don't know if M was sleeping or just pretending to, but she was on her side in her bed with her back to the door. She didn't speak or move and I got what I needed and hustled back out.

My mom helped me tuck a large sheet around the bottom of the couch and I can fold it over onto my body when I go to sleep. There's a stack of blankets at the foot of the old leather couch, and an antique, blue glass lamp my dad bought forever ago at some antique store glows softly from the corner. The radiator is pumping out warm air, and the house smells of the butter and lemon from the pound cake, which is cooling on the counter. The pale pink sheet is old, familiar, soft, and smells like the fabric softener my mom loves. I can hear the fog horns in the distance, low and sad. Despite the mess of my life in general, I feel a moment of blissful content. A feeling of pure home goodness. Even with sleeping on the couch and being basically forced out of my own room, I feel comfy-cozy and private. Ryan is in his room studying, and my parents are in the dining room going over bills.

I am just about to brush my teeth when the phone rings. It's nine-thirty. I grab it quickly, suspecting it might be Nicki. I really can be psychic sometimes, honestly.

"Hello?" I speak quietly.

"Ariel?" Yep, it's Nicki. She's talking quietly.

"Hi, Nick," I say in a normal voice. My mom pokes her head around the corner just then and taps her wrist meaningfully. I tell Nicki just a second, and say to Mom, "It's Nicki, about something for school, we won't be on long."

Mom is satisfied and leaves.

"Okay I'm back, but I can't talk long," I tell Nicki.

Nicki whispers back, "I am sneaking this call, Ariel—you know my parents don't want me on the phone after 9:00. But I have to talk to you. M called me, earlier. She's really upset about what you said today, Ariel. I mean, she doesn't want to live with you anymore! She might leave, go back to her mom! You have to make up!" Nicki is speaking in a rush. She might get caught and forced off the phone at any moment, and she is also uncomfortable being drawn into conflict. She's a peace-girl, so I know this is stressing her out in a huge way, probably almost as much as me and M, who are actually *in* it.

"Nicki, honestly, I don't think I did anything wrong."

Uncomfortable silence. Obviously *she* does.

"*You're* the one who thought she was too shy to interview," I point out.

Nicki sighs. She sounds way older than she is. "I know, but I didn't mean it like she took it. I meant it to be, you know, recognizing that she doesn't usually get into stuff that is so . . . so . . . not for shy people!" Nicki's voice is getting louder as she explains to me. I know exactly how Nicki meant it, I know she only meant to be kind and thoughtful, and it's not nice of me to be pulling her through the wringer like this. I interrupt her.

"I know, Nick, sorry. I know you were just trying to be nice. But M, well, she's taken over my room now, pretending to be sick, so I can't really go make up with her just now." I become sarcastic near the end of this. I can't possibly explain to Nicki all the Meadow stuff, the way my family is around M, why this is all under my skin.

"I know. She told me. After I apologized to her." This is said with a tone that says like-*you*-should-apologize. "She really does want to leave, Ariel. *You have got to make up*," Nicki tells me in her best bossy voice.

But it isn't simple anymore. It's not a matter of us saying, "Sorry," "Okay," "We're best buddies again" and moving on. It's more like a piece of china that broke into a bunch of little pieces. No matter how carefully the pieces are reassembled and glued, the cracks will always show. It will never be as it first was. When you know this you feel like there's no point even collecting the pieces and trying to put them back together.

"If she leaves, she leaves," I tell Nicki. "There's nothing I can do about it."

Nicki huffs out a breath of surprise. "Yes you *can*, Ariel! Say sorry, make up, go back to being best friends!"

"But I'm not sorry, and we can't go back." It's not exactly true that I am not sorry, but I am not ready to admit this.

"But she'll leave us!" Nicki is tearful.

"Well, then, she will," I sound much more cool and uncaring then I feel.

"Ariel! We all worked so hard to get her to stay with you. It makes no sense."

She wants to pin this on me? Well, I have a question for her. "Nicki, where were *you* after the meeting tonight?"

She coughs delicately, and then says, "What do you mean?"

"I called like two hours after the meeting and your mom said you weren't home yet. You can't have stayed that long working. The janitor would have made you leave."

I wait. Nicki is silent.

"Nick, what's going on with you?"

"Ariel, let's just deal with you and M right now."

"So you're freezing me out."

Nicki's voice rises in alarm. "No! It's not like that, Air. It's nothing to do with you, I mean, there's nothing *up* really . . ."

"Okay, you're freezing me out."

Just then I hear Nicki's mom in the background. She tells me, "Look, I have to get off the phone. Ariel, everything's fine with me, it is you and M that I called to talk about. Fix this. Please?"

I start to pry more, ignoring her plea, but Nicki hurries off the phone after a quick good-bye.

I turn my head into the pillow and the tears come. I've just had it. When I finally do sleep, I dream of making stuffed pork tenderloin. It's a complicated recipe I made when M was sleeping over last summer, and she loved it so much she asked for my recipe so she and her mother could make it. She told me later that it was hard for them to make and it kind of fell apart. She was impressed that I was already like a real chef, and I had felt so good. I told her, when I put it in a cookbook some day, I would call it *Pork Tenderloin à la M.* She laughed and made me promise, which I did.

In my dream, we are eating this dish, but in the stuffing there is some ingredient that is sharp and hard to chew. We begin spitting out these tiny pieces of hard, plasticlike stuff. They are pictures, shaped into jigsaw pieces, miniature portraits of us when we were little—in the sandbox as grimy, diapered toddlers, dressed up as fairies from the preschool costume box, starting first grade with matching Care Bears backpacks, and walking the trail with Nicki recently, all of us wind-blown and carefree. We spit out the tiny, sharp-cornered pictures, each no bigger than a thumbtack, and grimly stuff them back into our mouths. The meat is delicious, but the pictures cut our mouths.

Stuffed Pork Tenderloin
à la M

2 pork tenderloins (pork tenderloin is usually sold in
      packs of 2, so you can make both, to feed over four
      people, or freeze one, half this recipe, and use it later,
      like M does when it is (was) just her and her mom)

6 slices bacon, chopped

½ C. diced, tart green apple (like Granny Smith)

¼ C. diced celery

¼ C. diced onion

2 C. bread, preferably slightly stale white bread from a
      leftover baguette torn into little pieces (You can use
      any bread you have, but if it's fresh, turn the oven on
      to 200° and put the bread in for a few minutes, until
      it gets dried out.)

¼ C. chicken broth

1 t. dried sage

½ t. ground nutmeg

salt and pepper

kitchen string or several uncooked spaghetti noodles

Preheat oven to 400°.

*Make stuffing: Cook chopped bacon in a skillet until it is
crispy. Set aside; try not to snack on it. Pour the bacon grease
into a coffee mug, leaving behind about a teaspoon in the pan.
(When you have extra grease, you can let it cool off and then
you can pour it in the trash. Don't put it in the sink because
it will make a grease clog and your dad will be really mad.*

*Don't pour it straight into the trash either because it'll melt
the plastic trash bag and make a hole for the other trash to
fall out of, also making your dad really mad.) Cook the apples,
celery, and onion in the reserved pan, about 5 minutes, until
soft. Add chicken broth, bring it to a boil, and add bread and
herbs. Cook and stir until most of liquid is gone, and bread is
golden but still soft, about another 5 minutes. Set aside.*

*To prepare the tenderloins: remove from packaging and
rinse with cool water, dry well with paper towels. Using a
sharp, narrow knife, remove the "silver skin" (the whitish, thin
membrane) by slipping the blade under this skin and pulling/
cutting to separate it. Also remove and throw away any visible
fat. Carefully split the tenderloin with your knife long-ways.
Don't cut all the way through—when you have cut almost all
the way through, stop and lay the sides back as though you are
opening a book. This is called "butterflying."*

*Assemble: Put one half of the stuffing (or all of it if you have
halved this recipe and are working with only one tenderloin)
on one side of each of the butterflied loins. Fold the other half
of the meat over the stuffing, enclosing it. Use your fingers
to press and seal the seams together. Cut several lengths of
cooking string and use them to hog-tie the loins in three or
four places. (If you don't have string, you can use uncooked
spaghetti, broken into toothpick-sized lengths, to skewer the
seams closed. The pasta will cook and soften in the juices,
becoming edible, so no need to remove after cooking.) Tuck in
the ends also, so stuffing doesn't leak out. Place tenderloins
in 13x9" baking dish coated with cooking spray, seam side*

down. Brush top of loins with reserved bacon fat. Cook for 25 to 35 minutes, depending on thickness of rolls. Meat should be nicely browned and sizzling. Let rest 5 minutes before cutting off string. Slice into rounds to serve.

Plans for Peace

Despite sleeping on the couch and all this stress, I slept heavily and my dreams were vivid, but then I sunk into a deep, dark, black sleep. Now I feel rested. I need to grab a quick shower before school, but don't want to run into M. I am folding the sheet I slept on when my mom comes in, yawning and scratching at her arm, freshly awake.

"Morning, honey." She grabs the dangling end of the sheet and we fold it into progressively smaller squares, working smoothly and quickly, just as we do on laundry day.

"Our couch is more comfortable for sleeping than I thought it would be," I pat a cushion, "but I still think I earned coffee . . ." She lets me drink coffee just every once in awhile, like on New Year's Day when we have stayed up late. She thinks it stunts growth, and I don't need any more strikes against me in that department. I love coffee though, and will risk staying short to drink it. I am always trying to work out an angle to weasel a morning cup out of her.

She considers, yawning again. "Okay, Air, for your kindness in giving up your room to a sick friend, I do think you deserve a cuppa."

It wasn't exactly kindness, I think with a bit of guilt, but I just smile and rub my hands together in anticipation of caffeine. "Have you seen M today, Mom?"

"Actually, I did, just now. She was going to the bathroom. I think I startled her, because when I came around the corner she looked like she was about to bolt back to your room or something."

So she's avoiding me too. This is some sort of craziness, trying to live in the same house without seeing each other.

"She still sick?"

"She is. Worse. She has circles under her eyes. I don't think she slept much. She's staying home today."

Well that's a relief. I'm sure she'll hide out until I leave for school. I can get to the bathroom without treating it like a mission through a war zone. I put what I hope is a look of concern for my friend in place and tell Mom I'm heading to the shower. She goes to the kitchen to make the coffee.

The morning passes quickly. I'm not like M, who doesn't have to pay close attention or study much. I need to take notes and do all the practice exercises, plus study at home. I want As and Bs. Actually I have to get As and Bs or my parents cut back on how much free time I get to watch cooking shows and experiment in the kitchen.

I have been envious of M's ease at school since kindergarten, when she was already reading *Arthur* books while I was still struggling with *Henry and Mudge.* Throughout the years it's been like this—she is just a whiz at school. She scarcely even tries, and doesn't much care about the streams of straight As that march across her report cards. She has other issues. She has always wanted to be more outgoing and social, and has always been jealous of the way I am naturally confident and can talk to almost anyone. And I don't blush. We have said many times that if we could mash the two of us into one girl, she would be nearly perfect: brainy, outgoing, and physically perfectly portioned. Balanced. She has totally destroyed all that—she's unbalanced everything. I feel a fresh surge of anger.

Right now, for the first time, I am almost relieved that pre-algebra is so hard for me. I am barely scraping out a B in this class, and I need to focus. I can't rely on M's help with it now. Struggling to understand these equations leaves me no room for any other thoughts, and right now that's a good thing.

Nicki finds me as soon as I come out of the classroom. "Did you bring your lunch today?" she asks me.

"Nope, I didn't. I didn't have time this morning to make anything."

"Me either, guess it's cafeteria slop then?"

I nod glumly. Calling the cafeteria food "slop" is not an exaggeration. It is, literally, something that should only be put in a pig's trough. We eat it as a last resort because it's better than extreme hunger, which is the only other option.

We line up and grab red plastic trays, sliding them along the rail in front of the food stations. Nicki takes a piece of limp pizza. The cheap pepperoni has curled into little cups that hold suspicious red oil. I go for the spaghetti, even though the sauce is super-sweet and the bizarre neon color is a slap in the face of real tomatoes everywhere. I don't understand how people can make this kind of food for kids in schools. Do they think we don't have taste buds or that we like tons of grease and sugar and no texture? I could go on. This is why I al- most always bring my own food.

We head outside, grabbing the end of a bench in the shade. Nicki uses napkins to soak up the grease from the pepperoni. At least our little cartons of milk are ice cold.

"Did you and M finally talk?"

"No. She's camped out in *my* room, apparently super sick."

"This is out of control, Ariel. You know it."

I play with my spaghetti, not looking at Nicki. "Yeah, I'll give you that, Nick, it is."

"Well, you were mean yesterday. You should say sorry."

"I feel like I was *truthful,* Nicki."

Nicki begins the hair twisting that is her signature stress gesture. "Okay, so maybe she's obsessing about being Meadow. But so what? Why is it such a, *a thing*?"

I consider Nicki's question, and I don't feel any more like I can even answer it.

"Ariel, you know you are stubborn. You say it enough about yourself. And your family is so cool and close and all that. You're so lucky that way. Seems like M has somehow made you feel, I don't know, threatened?"

"Honestly I don't even know, Nick. At first it was just so annoying the way she was so caught up in doing Dad's commercials. I mean I like *The Sopranos,* but I don't want to watch episodes back to back, pausing as Meadow says something so M can write down that her left lip quivers or whatever. And my family is trying too hard to make it a big deal too. It's not just the commercials either . . . it's, I don't know, everything just started to be different. Like, she doesn't get our family jokes and stuff, so we have stopped telling them. Now at dinner we only talk about *The Sopranos* and the ads. At first I was so worried about her feeling out of place, and I would try to stop my family from doing quirky stuff, and then they did. I hated it. There's so much little stuff, but it's big somehow too, if that makes sense. Like

M hates what she calls 'artificial smells' so my mom took out all the little Glade room scent thingies that smell so great. When I walk into the house it doesn't even *smell* like my house anymore."

As I speak I feel an understanding of this whole thing slowly dawning on me. I believe it is what people mean when they say "the big picture," the way I am seeing this. I don't like M living with me, how it makes my life different. It is absurdly simple.

Nicki gives voice to my realization. "So M living with you isn't what you thought it would be, okay."

I nod slowly, feeling the tears starting to well up. It is ironic that I am the one who pushed for her to come and live with us, and now I hate it. I am the one who practically forced her to watch *The Sopranos*, and now I hate that she loves it. She brought game night back to us and made my family tighter, but that's suddenly stopped too. What a mess.

Nicki interrupts my thoughts. "So okay then, tell her, talk to her, Ariel. It's not too late to work this out! There are seven months left in the year, that's it. You guys can work it out until then, Air. Say sorry, tell her you miss the Glade, whatever!" Nicki is chattering quickly now, so eager to form a plan for this make-up.

I think Nicki's right. It *is* hard to let go of my anger and resentment, to admit I haven't been very nice. I know I am stubborn. I say, "Okay, yeah, you're mostly right I guess, but I think M needs to own *part* of it too. I mean, the Meadow thing really is overblown."

Nicki nods, smiling, delighted to see an end to this drama. "Yeah, sure, but you can talk it out. You love each other, you're best friends. You can!" Hand the girl some pom-poms and she'd burst into a cheer.

"Do you want to come over after school, help me talk to M? You know, be our 'voice of reason'?" I am suddenly anxious not to face M alone.

"Absolutely," Nicki says, as she balls up the grease-soaked napkins and stuffs them into her milk carton. The pizza sits uneaten on her tray. "And maybe we can make that yummy artichoke dip M loves? Remember, you made it last summer after she had the huge fight with her mom? You called it 'Achy Breaky Artichoke Hearts Dip.' It made M laugh so hard she stopped crying."

I remember. "Yeah, we can make that after we talk, and I have these yummy tortilla chips that'll be perfect with it." I am happy now. It's a relief to have a plan and it feels good to have a dish to seal the deal. I can't wait to be back in with M again. Now that I really think about it, I miss her. We have never in our lives been so separate as we have been since she moved in. I am still mad, but we can talk it out.

Achy Breaky
Artichoke Hearts Dip

1 can marinated artichoke hearts, drained and chopped
¾ C. mayonnaise
1 small can diced Ortega chilies
1 C. grated parmesan cheese
1 T. lemon juice
½ t. sugar
dash of pepper

Combine all the ingredients in a bowl, mix well. Bake in a small, ovenproof dish at 375° for 45 minutes, or until golden and bubbly. Dip tortilla chips, breadsticks, fresh veggies, etc.

Gone

Lunch period is almost over, and Nicki and I have been mostly quiet since I agreed to begin peace talks with M.

"So, Nick, you might want to eat something. The bell is about to ring," I point to the untouched tray of food sitting in front of her. I also notice how thin she looks. She really hasn't been eating much lately now that I think about it.

She shakes her head a bit, her eyes refocusing. "Huh?"

I point to her plastic fork, then to her mouth, "We earthlings do this thing called eating . . . try it!" I pick a pepperoni slice from her pizza and make a big show of chewing it.

Nicki smiles. She grabs the fork and stabs it into the fruit cocktail. She looks for a long moment at the pastel fruit, and then drops the fork back onto the tray. "Eww. This stuff is disgusting. Look, the grapes are *gray*."

"And the cherries are neon. You're right, that's fruit gone wrong. But you should eat . . ."

She shakes her head and shoves the tray away. "I'm fine, actually." She arches her back into a cat stretch and closes her eyes briefly. "I don't feel like eating."

"Okay. Then can we talk about what's up with *you* lately?"

"Nothing! God, don't worry about *me* right now."

She is, literally, saved from further interrogation by the bell ending lunchtime. I have a feeling I wouldn't have gotten anything out of her anyway. Maybe there isn't anything to get, I just don't know.

Finally, the last bell of the day. Nicki and I gather our things from our lockers quickly, anxious to get to my house. On the walk there, Nicki counsels me not to go into a "stubborn zone" if M happens to irritate me about the Meadow ads, or whatever. I say things like "yes ma'am" and I salute her as she lectures. She's got a lot of common sense, so while I am making fun of her, I am also taking her advice very seriously.

When we get home, M is in the kitchen. She doesn't say anything to me, but nods to Nicki.

My parents aren't here and Ryan's at practice, so there's no reason we can't just get right into it here and now.

"M, look, I am sorry I was rotten about the Meadow

role. About a lot of stuff. We need to talk about everything, I know it's all gotten so out of hand, and . . ."

M gives me what I can only call a cold look, interrupting and standing up abruptly as she says, "I'm leaving, Ariel. Obviously you don't want me here. My mom already bought me a plane ticket and I fly out of San Francisco on Saturday."

She brushes past me and goes in my/our room and slams the door.

— —

Nicki and I are frozen for a moment. Speechless. Nicki is the first to process what M has just told us, and says, "I'll go talk to her, stay here."

I nod, bite my lip and taste blood, and fall back into a chair. M is leaving? This morning I think I would have seen that as welcome news, but now it makes me feel terrible. I wonder if I should go talk to her too. No, I decide, Nicki will handle it, come tell me when it's okay. I sit, frozen, waiting. But I don't know what I'm waiting for.

Fifteen minutes pass, and finally Nicki comes out, trailed by M. I wait. I can feel my armpits sweating and my heart is beating a little too fast.

M sits across from me. "Nicki told me you were going to apologize today."

I nod. "I know we need to talk about how this all got to be so complicated . . ."

M cuts me off. "You know, I don't want to, Ariel. It's done. I called my mom awhile ago and told her I was miserable living apart from her, so she thinks that's why I'm leaving. And I told your mom the same thing this morning. They all bought it. But I want you to know that I am leaving because of *you*, Ariel."

It is the meanest, truest thing M has ever said to me. I start to shake. "M, no, please, I know I haven't been cool. It's not you, exactly. It's a bunch of little stuff I think, that piled up on me. My family has been different, and—"

"Do you think it is *easy for me*, living here? Do you know what it's like watching you all 'Uncle John' each other? Telling all your inside jokes? Trying to be the polite houseguest all the time? Wondering if I am in the way? Feeling alone? Your parents are great, but they aren't *mine*, Ariel. I am tired of it all . . . sick to death of trying so hard here, with you."

All three of us have tears running down our faces. Nicki is rubbing M's back. I don't know what to say. I don't know how to fix this. The only thing I can think of is her Meadow obsession. If I can get her to stay until next week maybe I can talk her out of actually leaving.

I say, "But what about being Meadow? The shoot is next week for both commercials. Why don't you at least stay until then, for that? I mean, my dad is counting on you!"

"You be Meadow, Ariel. Or whatever. Remember, it's just stupid, local cable? Not a big deal?"

"I'm sorry, M. I am *so* sorry I said all that." I am practically whispering. I feel so ashamed. "Can you forgive me?"

M pauses a long time. I realize this might have gone to a place we can't come back from. On some level I always thought, no matter what happened, no matter how big the fight, no matter how cutting the words, M and I would always, ultimately, come back to our best friendship. I always took that, maybe even her, for granted. I see now, maybe too late, that we are fragile.

"Sure, Ariel, I forgive you." M says it flatly. "I have to go pack."

Nicki asks quietly, "Is there any chance you'll change your mind, Mattie? I'll miss you so much, and I need you for the yearbook . . ."

M shakes her head. Her eyes are so sad. "Can you come say good-bye before I leave on Saturday?"

Nicki is crying too hard to speak, but nods.

M goes back to our room.

— —

It's Saturday. Nicki got here a little while ago, keeping her promise to see M off. My dad is driving M to the airport in five minutes. He's loading her stuff in the car. We are keeping her furniture until her mom can drive down for it, probably at spring break. Nicki and I wanted to go to the airport to see her off, but M said it would be too hard saying good-bye at the airport. My parents said that was understandable, thinking M is so heart-broken to be leaving us. They have no idea what's really going on—they think we've been acting mopey and weird just because she's leaving.

All the mad went out of both of us, I think, after the blowout. We spent the rest of this week being strangely civil to each other, but we did not talk again about anything deeper then coordinating shower schedules. Game night resumed, but no one had any enthusiasm anymore, and we ended up abandoning two games only half-played. At night we each lay in our beds, now separated so that they are on opposite walls, quiet, until we fell asleep. There isn't anything left to say. M is closed down and shut off, so there's no use even trying.

She told my parents, last night at dinner, that her mom's agoraphobia is flaring up and she has missed several days of work at her new job. M said this is part of the reason she needs to go. I don't know if it's true or not. If it is, I feel a teeny bit less guilty because maybe I am not the only reason she is leaving. Then again, if her mom really is going downhill, I feel awful for M, having to move to a new place, start a new school, *and* worry about her mom's mental issues. See? Anything to do with M is so complicated and sad right now.

My dad comes in from outside, where he has finished loading the last of M's stuff into the trunk. "You ready to go, Mattie?"

"Yep." She grabs her backpack. "Well, this is it." She hugs Nicki first, holding on for a minute and patting her back. They let go, but first they briefly grab hands. Then she comes over to me and hugs me briefly. A show for my dad. There is no eye contact and her body is totally stiff. She said bye to my mom and Ryan earlier—they had to leave for a scrimmage game—and they both got real hugs too.

Last night I couldn't sleep, thinking about this moment, the grand exit. Finally, at about two in the morning, I got up and went to the den. I decided to write M a letter to read on the plane. I wrote for two hours. I poured out everything, even about the Glade room fresheners and how I really was jealous of her playing Meadow. About how unfair that was because I could have been in any of my dad's commercials but I hadn't wanted to. As I wrote, I realized I was writing to myself in a way too, unwinding each thread that had become part of this huge tangle between us, laying it out flat, looking at it, and moving on to the next part. I wrote about how much she means to me, about how I have realized that she is a huge part of my life, my past, and hopefully my future. I told her how, thanks to her, Solomon Family Game Night had reconnected my family. I wrote until my hand ached and my fingertips were numb. I wrote until the sun was just starting to come up. I didn't reread any of it when I finished, just sealed it in an envelope and wrote "Mattie-M-Matilda" on the front.

I went in the kitchen then, and made a tuna sandwich to remind her how far we go back. M once called me the "tuna sandwich miracle worker." Back in fourth grade, M forgot her lunch one day and I volunteered to split my tuna sandwich with her. She had claimed to hate tuna, but I had insisted she try *my* tuna sandwich. Long story short, she did, she loved it, and to this day she will not eat tuna unless it's my "Miracle Tuna."

I make the sandwich quickly, wrap it in plastic, then in foil. I don't want it to smell, I want it to be fresh, and I want her to be surprised. I put a small ice pack into a plastic shopping bag with the sandwich. I tape the letter to the bag, tie it closed, and bury it in M's backpack, underneath a dirty sweatshirt in a side pocket I know she hardly ever uses. I asked my dad to tell her while they are driving to the airport to check that pocket of her backpack once she is on the plane, that I had put a good-bye note in it. He promised he would.

I watch the car round the corner, catching a last glimpse of M in the passenger seat. Her head is tilted toward my dad as she listens to something he must be saying. Then she is gone.

Tuna Miracle
Sandwich

1 can albacore tuna, packed in water

2 T. plain yogurt

1 T. capers

1 T. chopped dill pickle

pinch of sugar

dash of pepper

2 slices sourdough bread, lightly toasted

1 t. mayonnaise

lettuce leaves

1 slice Swiss cheese

paper-thin sliced tomatoes

Empty tuna into a colander and use the back of a spoon to squeeze out all the water. Tuna should be almost dry and crumbly. In a small bowl, mix the tuna and yogurt with a fork, breaking up the tuna and mixing until there are no large chunks left. Add capers, pickles, sugar and pepper. Mix well. To assemble: spread mayonnaise thinly on both pieces of bread. Line one slice with lettuce leaves, pack tuna onto lettuce, lay tomatoes over tuna, then put the cheese over the tomato. Finish with another layer of lettuce before capping with the other slice of sourdough. Having lettuce next to the bread on both sides makes a barrier and keeps the bread from getting soggy. M says that is the fatal flaw in tuna sandwiches—soggy bread.

Ryan's Story

It's Sunday night. I am still waiting, hoping, to hear from M. I need to know if the letter made any difference. She did call yesterday to say she had arrived safely, but only my mom talked to her.

I slept really late this morning, read and dozed some, but I still feel tired and unable to commit to an activity. By activity I mean washing my hair, painting my toenails, or maybe even tackling the huge task of collecting all the dirty clothes on my floor and schlepping them to the washing machine . . . all things I planned to do today. Instead I have been a slug. I watched *Married to the Mob* on Lifetime and then *The Departed* on Showtime. And that was the most active part of my day. Pathetic!

School is going to be weird without M. I still can't believe she really left. Nicki had to go to San Jose for a family get-together, and she's not coming back until Tuesday, so tomorrow I really will be alone. I am considering this fact when Ryan leans in my doorway and surveys my room. Besides the clothes, there are at least three dirty water glasses, cooking magazines spread out all over the floor near my bed, and a fairly impressive jumble of cosmetics and hair stuff on my dresser. My dad moved M's bed and dresser to the garage last night, and my mess has somehow sprawled into that space already—it's like M never even lived here.

"You are a pig, Ariel." Ryan shakes his head, using his toe to nudge a wadded-up wet towel.

Of course, the pig reference immediately makes me think of M. Again. "Shut up, Ryan."

"Ah, I'm just messing with you, no pun intended." See what I mean about our family's sense of humor? Ryan laughs, thoroughly pleased with his wit.

I sigh, flopping back on my pillow. "I know, Ry, I'm just in a bad mood."

"'Cause M left?"

"Yeah." I don't want to tell Ryan about why she really left.

"Too bad, about it, huh?"

I nod. "Ryan? Remember that night at dinner when I first asked Mom and Dad to consider having M come live with us?"

"Uh-huh."

"Why did you work so hard to convince them it was

a good idea? I mean, I was so glad then, and I know Mom and Dad were really swayed by what you said, but I never understood why. I know you like M okay and all that . . ."

Ryan steps into my room and slides down the wall, sitting with his back against it and his long legs sticking out. "Do you remember, about two summers ago, when I was trying to start that band with Chad and Evan?"

"More or less." I vaguely remember Ryan and his two friends clearing a space in the garage and trying to play used electric guitars. They were awful and I think they gave up on it pretty quickly.

"The guys were here one day, to practice, and my stomach was hurting. M was over here that day too."

I don't know where this is going, but I wait for him to continue.

"I remember, you were making those Thousand Dollar Cookies. The ones with that story about the lady who bought them at Macy's?"

"*Million* Dollar Cookies, and it was Neiman Marcus." I correct him automatically.

"Okay, whatever. The point is that you guys were here, in the kitchen. My friends were in the living room waiting for me, and I was just about to join them. I was in the hall, when I, uh, had an accident." Ryan is looking down and a scarlet blush is blooming up his neck and over his cheeks.

I am confused. "An accident?"

He looks up, obviously embarrassed. "I crapped my-self, okay, Ariel?"

"Oh! *That* kind of accident." Geez, didn't see that coming.

"Yeah, that kind. I think I had a stomach flu or something. And the only way I could get to the bath-room would be through the living room. Ariel, it was really gross, and I stood there, knowing it must show, and it was starting to smell, and my friends were there calling me. I was so humiliated I wanted to die. Then I looked up and M was standing in the hall on the kitchen side. I knew she saw it and knew what had hap-pened. She stared at me for a second, and she looked, I don't know, *understanding,* I guess.

"Without saying anything, she walked into the living room and asked Chad and Evan if they could come outside to unstick the kitchen window. She said you couldn't get it unstuck and you were hot because of the cookies in the oven. The window wasn't stuck, you know, she knows, that window is painted closed and not meant to open. She was just getting them out of there so I could get to the bathroom and into my room for new clothes. She made me an escape route, basically."

"I never knew any of this."

"I know, Air. And I thought she would tell you about it, but she just went on making cookies after that, and I guess she didn't. I got cleaned up and changed my clothes and came back through the kitchen, expecting you to comment, but I could tell you didn't know."

"She never said anything."

"That's the kind of thing that can ruin you. Like kids calling you 'crap-pants' or whatever for the rest of your life?"

"That's why you wanted her to come and live with us?"

He rubs his hands back and forth over his hair. "I felt like I could sort of, I don't know, return a favor or something."

"Yeah, I can see that."

"I was embarrassed around her for awhile after that, but she never brought it up or anything. I was grateful for that."

Suddenly I realize that Ryan is almost a man. Well, he's not a boy anymore. His shoulders are broad, and he has actual beard stubble. I feel off-kilter as I become aware of this, as if this whole transition has happened in the last five minutes. I also realize he's told me something really, really personal. He's trusted me. It's been a long time since me and Ryan were this honest with each other.

"And, Ariel, she was fun. I thought I was done play-ing games with you guys, but it was cool, while she was here, all of us hanging out like that. I miss it." He looks a little embarrassed admitting this. I need to tell him the truth.

"Ryan?"

"Hmm?"

"I liked those game nights too. And, you should know something . . . M didn't leave because of her mom. It was me."

"What do you mean?"

I tell him all of it, finishing with the letter and the fact that I haven't heard from her since she left.

He whistles long and low when I finish. "Geez, Ariel. That's harsh."

I nod glumly.

Ryan starts rubbing his head again, thinking through my story. Finally he says, "What is the one thing that made her really, really happy?"

I shrug. I don't know what he means.

"It's being Meadow and doing Dad's commercials. She was on fire about that."

Until I stomped it into the ground, I think.

"But she's gone now, Ryan. It's too late. Dad's going to have Ms. Slater's niece be—"

Ryan cuts me off. "How much money do you have?"

"Huh?"

"I think there might be a way for you to salvage this whole deal."

Million Dollar
Cookies

The story is that a lady ate in a café at Neiman Marcus, and got a cookie. She loved it and asked if she could buy the recipe. The waitress told her she could, for "two-fifty." When the woman got her credit card bill, she had been charged $250.00, and the department store wouldn't issue her a credit when she complained. As revenge she emailed the recipe to everyone she could think of, so that tons of people could have the recipe free. I did a report for social studies on this, investigated whether it was an "urban legend" or not, and found out that this never actually happened. Neiman Marcus doesn't have a café, or sell recipes. It's still a great story though, and these cookies are to die for.

(Recipe makes over 100 cookies, but can be halved.)

2 C. butter, softened	4 eggs
2 C. sugar	2 t. vanilla
2 C. brown sugar	4 C. flour

5 C. blended oatmeal (use blender or food-processor
    to blend until very fine)

1 t. salt	2 t. baking soda
2 t. baking powder	24 oz. chocolate chips

1 (8 oz.) Hershey bar grated (freeze the bar before grating)

3 C. chopped nuts

Preheat oven to 375°. Blend butter and both kinds of sugar with an electric mixer until creamy. Add eggs and vanilla, and mix until well-blended. Mix together with flour, oatmeal, salt, baking powder, and baking soda. The dry ingredients are very hard to mix together but worth the trouble when you taste the cookie. Add chips and grated chocolate. Add nuts last, mix. Roll into walnut sized balls. Place 2 inches apart on a cookie sheet. Bake for 6 to 8 minutes or until just barely starting to brown. Let cookies sit on baking sheet for 2 minutes before moving them to cooling racks.

And . . . Action!

I thought my dad's commercials were probably shot
by some guy with a digital camera, not a crew of five
people rushing around moving lights and holding
microphones on long poles. It is surprising how professional they all are. The gray-haired lady with the
headset actually has one of those sign things with the
bar to slam down when she says "cut" or "action." It
reads, "Island Sweets—Cable 9 v53-4" on a dry erase
strip across the top. Each time the lady yells "cut" and
they have to do it again—because something went
wrong—she changes the last number. Each re-do is
called a "take."

The ad is getting filmed in a car, from the front. The
windshield has been removed to avoid reflections when
filming people in a car. My dad sits in the driver's seat
and he has a tight, rubber head thing on with a fringe of

fake hair ringing the bottom—it makes him look bald like Tony Soprano. He wears a button-down Hawaiian shirt, just like Tony wears on the show, and his already large stomach has been padded beneath the shirt. It practically touches the steering wheel it is so huge. From a distance, he actually does look a lot like James Gandolfini, the actor who plays Tony.

But M is stealing the show. She could be the body double for Jamie-Lynn Sigler, the girl who plays Meadow. She wears the "Meadowhead" wig my dad bought for her all those weeks ago, and the long, dark brown length is swept into a perfect, Meadow-like pony tail. She wears the contact lenses my mom bought her to change her hazel eyes to a deep brown, and as she says her lines she holds them open, giving her the doe-eyed look of Meadow. I have watched the episodes M used to "study" Meadow so many times that I know how incredibly close M is coming to look-ing, sounding, acting, and moving just like Meadow. She's dead on.

They filmed the first spot this morning, the one with the "chocolate contraband." I couldn't watch that one because there wasn't room in the little room they used as a set. It was in a model home that is still under construc-tion, and my dad borrowed furniture from a store in Oakland to make it look fancy, like the Sopranos' house in the show. Anyway, M and Dad both said it went well. At least I get to watch one of the ads get made.

The director yells "action" again. This is their fifth try. The commercial is loosely based on an episode from season one called "College." In this scene, Meadow and her dad are driving to visit colleges, and she confronts him about being in the mafia. Tony admits to gambling and some petty crimes, but not to the truth, which is that he is actually a crime boss. Then, when he is at Bowdoin College with Meadow, he sees a quote on the wall that really hits him because of the way he has just lied to Meadow. It is part of a Nathaniel Hawthorne poem that reads, "No man . . . can wear one face to himself, and another to the multitude, without finally getting bewildered as to which may be the true."

The commercial M and Dad are filming is loosely based on this episode. In the ad M says to my dad (aka Tony Soprano), "Is it true, Dad, that you are a criminal? That you make money because of your involvement in 'dark' things?" She says "dark" in a sinister way, and nails Meadow's slightly nasal, East-coast accent.

They banter for a few sentences, lifted directly from the episode, until Dad-slash-Tony finally says, in an over-done Jersey accent, "Okay, already, Meadow. It's true, it's true, I make my living with *dark* things . . . dark chocolate truffles, dark chocolate fudge cups, and dark chocolate dipped apples. I even give innocent children free dark chocolate lava cake on their birthdays!"

M-slash-Meadow looks out the window with a stunned, tragic look on her face. In the final version of the commercial, the highly recognizable music that plays during the opening credits of *The Sopranos* will start up just as M looks out the window, and on the bottom of the screen they'll have the Hawthorne quote rewritten to say: "No man (or woman) can eat just one Island Sweets dark chocolate truffle and then one Island Sweets signature mocha truffle without finally being bewildered as to which one is better." Then they'll show the license plate of the car, which will say "I M 4 Chclte" surrounded by little guns.

The fifth take is a keeper. The cable crew announces we are finished and they start to pack up. Dad peels off the rubber skull cap and rubs his hands through his own thin, graying hair. M hops out of the car and saunters over to me.

"Whattaya think, Ariel?" She is anxious to hear my opinion.

"You were awesome, M, seriously good. Perfect. I bet Jamie-Lynne Sigler will hear about this and hire you to be her double."

M giggles.

"Nicki was going to wait for us at the store, we should head over. My mom is over there now too, she wants to take pictures of you as Meadow. And we can snag some chocolate, of course!"

"*Daaaark* chocolate," M says.

I laugh. It is supremely great to be laughing together again.

— —

She almost didn't come back. Here's how we persuaded her to return for the filming. After I told Ryan about everything, he said he had an idea. He suggested I buy a plane ticket for M to come back and do the commercials. I told him there was no way she would come back, that she was seriously pissed at me. But Ryan suggested we call M's mom and tell her it would be a surprise, from our parents, and ask her if she would be willing to cooperate and be in on it.

I had called their house right then. Her mom answered on the first ring, like she was expecting someone else. She sounded disappointed that it was only me and she told me right away that M was gone, walking on the beach. It was the perfect opportunity to lay out the plan. First I asked her how she was doing (fine, glad to have M back, sorry it didn't work out). Then I told her how disappointed my dad was about M not playing Meadow in the upcoming commercials. I fibbed a bit here and told her my parents wanted to buy M a plane ticket, as a belated going-away gift, to come back and shoot the ads.

M's mom said no at first, tickets were over $300 and that was too much to accept. If her mom knew I was actually spending my own money—that that's almost exactly how much I have in my savings account from cooking contests—she never would have agreed. But finally, after I explained that it would be a favor to my dad too and a fantastic surprise because M had really looked forward to being Meadow, her mom finally agreed.

Ryan helped me buy the ticket online. We told our parents that *M's mom* wanted to fly her back as a surprise, that it was her idea to cheer M up about leaving Alameda so abruptly. Okay this part was a little more than fibbing, it was outright lying, but there was no other way to make it come together.

I learned later that M's mom told her the "happy" news about the surprise trip to shoot the ads just last night. M had refused to come at first, but her mom pointed out that my dad was counting on her, and also the ticket, all $338, was already bought and non-refundable. M, thinking it was my parent's money, felt trapped by that, which is what Ryan said would push her into coming. And he was right. Her mom thought M's hesitation about coming back was all about leaving *her.* We had to work a different set of "facts" for each person to get M here, and I couldn't have pulled it off without Ryan's superior ability to create believable lies. He's frighteningly good at this.

M landed in San Francisco this morning looking bewildered. I waved cheerily, and she waved back limply, a look of confusion on her face.

When we were walking to the car, M had started to thank my dad for the ticket, but I interrupted, saying, "You mean helping your mom plan her surprise . . ."

M looked at me like I was crazy, but just mumbled something about big surprises and turbulence. I gave her a grateful look, and my dad let it go, thankfully.

Once we got back to my house, I dragged M, literally, into my room. I hugged her super hard while she stood there, stiff, and told her about Ryan helping me get her here. I could tell she was really impressed that we went to such lengths, and also that I spent all my cooking money on the ticket. I could see her start to melt—her eyes began to soften, and she looked right at me as I told her everything. She stopped avoiding eye contact. Finally, the hard, angry line of her mouth relaxed and curled into a cautious smile.

I felt an actual physical sensation of relief blossom deep in my belly. M admitted that my letter had really affected her, and she had already forgiven me in her heart, but still had some leftover anger hanging around in her brain. The last of it drained away, she said, as we were talking. We both admitted to feeling somewhat damaged, sort of scarred I guess, from this whole thing. I don't know how that can be undone, but hopefully time will do the trick.

Finally, she squeezed my hand and said, "Okay then, I've got some Meadow to channel!"

"I can help you with the makeup." We headed into

the bathroom then, and spent the next hour turning M into Meadow and talking all about M's new home in Crescent City.

Now, as we walk toward my dad's store, I realize that M will leave again tomorrow, permanently. I push away this depressing thought as we walk through the door of Dad's store and see Nicki, my mom, Ryan, and a bunch of the employees stand up and start clapping. There are balloons tied to the front counter.

My dad isn't here yet—he had to finish up some stuff with the director—but when he gets here, we're going to have an early lunch. I made "Gabagool Platters" of finger foods (*gabagool* is Italian slang for something to eat; they say it in *The Sopranos*). I wanted it to feel festive and to carry the theme of the commercial, to draw out M's moment of "fame" for her. It's one more way I can try to make up to her.

Finally, my dad is here, and we all sit down together, digging into the platters of cold cuts and talking loudly. M is a bit quiet, mostly listening, and I think again, that she is leaving for good tomorrow. I feel sad, but there is a tiny, secret voice telling me something else: I know it is for the best.

Gabagool

1 bunch romaine lettuce

2 to 3 lbs of any or all of the following cured Italian meats
(look in the deli section of your supermarket for
these. Buy a small amount of each to sample and
figure out what you like if you are unfamiliar with
them): salami, pancetta, prosciutto, sopressa, coppa,
mortadella, or any other specialty cured meats you
might come across

½ lb. thin-sliced provolone

½ lb. mozzarella, cubed

1 can black olives

1 small jar green olives, stuffed with pimento or garlic

1 small jar pitted kalamata olives (again, you can experiment with different kinds of olives)

3 large tomatoes, sliced into thick rounds, and halved

½ C. baby carrots

several pepperoncini or other pickled peppers

¼ C. olive oil

3 T. red wine vinegar

½ t. dried Italian seasoning

salt and pepper

toothpicks

*This is enough to make about two large platters of finger
foods. If you don't have large platters, you can use a flat piece*

of cardboard cut from a box, and covered with foil. Wash and dry lettuce leaves and lay out as a "bed." Roll meats and cheese slices into little cylinders. Arrange them neatly on leaves. Lay out everything else on the platters, up to the peppers. Mix the oil, vinegar, and seasoning in a bowl with a whisk. Just before serving the platters, drizzle the dressing over everything. Serve with fresh bread or crackers. Put out toothpicks. This is not really a recipe exactly, and it is totally open for new and different types of cold cuts and vegetables. It is called antipasto too. That's just Italian for "before the main course," like an appetizer.

Recipe for a Normal Day

It is one o'clock in the morning. We stayed up late, all of us, having a last Solomon Family Game Night with M. We played Sorry!, Clue, and Apples to Apples. We all laughed and fought and, while we all had a blast, it was a little sad knowing it would be awhile before M was back stirring up game night for us again.

M and I are in my room. We are exhausted. It has been a really long day, but we are unwilling to sleep because there is so little time left. This is the real leaving. The way M rushed off before, hurt and angry, wasn't it. Now we are facing our separation the way we should. We can't stop talking—there is so much to get caught up on.

I yawn again and ask M, "Do you have to start school on Monday?"

"Tuesday. My mom says I can have Monday to recover from the weekend."

"Are you scared?"

"I am, but at the same time it is exciting. I can be M or Mattie or Matilda. No one knows me at all, and that's such a . . . I don't know, like an opportunity or something."

I totally get that, and feel a flicker of envy.

"But, yeah, it *is* scary."

"What time is your flight tomorrow?"

"Not until later afternoon. Like four I think."

"What do you want to do until then?" I ask.

"I want to have Nicki over and make crepes. You know, those ones you make to work off steam? When you were mad at James last year you made about fifty of them. Remember, you called them your crepes of wrath? I want to learn so I can make them when the new school is stressful."

"Okay, I'll teach you. Cool."

"Nicki too." M sounds happy as she speaks. "And when I get lonely up in Crescent City I'll make crepes and that'll help me."

I have told M before that making something complicated is a great way to simmer down when I am upset, and I am pleased she wants to try it for herself. Plus, I love teaching recipes, so it'll be fun. But it seems kind of like a boring way for her to spend her last day in Alameda, which I tell her.

"That's the *point*, though, Ariel! I want your mom to be singing off-key from the den and Fiesta to be tripping you because he keeps going to sleep on the kitchen floor. I want Nicki to be turning all the little spice jars in that rack so that their labels are facing exactly forward as the smoke alarm goes off. I want Ryan and his friends to come in and say snarky stuff to us."

"I can't guarantee my mom will sing or that Ryan will be around."

M interrupts me, "Oh, I know Air, obviously, I am just saying I want to have the last day feel like a normal day. I want to remember being a part of things here."

I am quiet a moment, thinking that the kind of day she just described is something we won't have after tomorrow. Days like that never seemed special, but now I see that they were.

"M, I really am sorry, about the way things went. I mean you were part of the family, and I know I ruined that."

"I was never part of your family, Ariel. I know that now. I couldn't be. No, don't feel bad about how this all ended up. I think I would have had to leave anyway. I never should have let Mom move up there alone."

I think about what she is saying, and I know she is right. Families are complicated. Mine, hers, everyone's.

"M?"

"Hmm." She sounds sleepy now.

I click off the reading light on my night stand and see her snuggle into the blankets we mounded on the floor to make her a bed. Her eyes are closed.

"Remember, in second grade when the class called us 'the twins' all the time because we were so inseparable?"

"Uh-huh."

"I still feel like that, that we are joined, and I don't think your moving will change that."

"I love you too, Air. Now let's sleep. We've got crepes to make tomorrow."

"Okay, good night."

"Good night."

— —

As it turned out, making crepes the next day was anything but boring. We had my iPod on shuffle and were just hanging out, making crepe batter. Nicki was typically quiet, whisking eggs, listening to me and M chat. Then, out of the blue, she started crying and beating the eggs like she wanted to kill them. M and I could only stare. It was very un-Nicki-like, this drama. And why? She met our eyes, and threw her whisk in the sink. She sank onto a barstool and started talking. And Nicki had a story to tell us.

"I am in love, and I have been keeping it a secret." M and I waited, both of us with our mouths hanging open stupidly. "I'm tired of sneaking around and lying."

I moved next to her, gently gathered her hair into a braid behind her back. "Okay, Nick, tell us everything."

And so she did. Nicki talked for a half hour and we

didn't have to coax or pry at all. Frequently she would slap a palm down on the counter, and her voice was jerky with those weird hiccups that crying can bring on. I made crepe after crepe, just listening, and M sat quietly beside her, rubbing her back once in awhile, smoothing back strands of hair that stuck to her wet cheeks.

Shortly before school had ended last year, Nicki's parents discovered that she had a second cell phone (not her "emergency phone"). That wasn't the problem. The problem was *who* Nicki had been talking to on the secret phone. And that's when Nicki told us her secret: her parents had moved to Alameda because Nicki had had an older boyfriend who they did not want her to see anymore. Cole, Nicki's guy, was Nicki's cousin's best friend. That's how they met; her cousin had brought Cole to a family reunion three summers ago. This cousin had also helped Nicki and this boyfriend secretly keep in touch all this time. Nicki had been lying to her parents (and to us), saying she was talking to her cousin whenever she got "caught," but she was really talking to her boyfriend, Cole.

M and I had to know the *whole* story, so she backed up and filled in the details. Cole was seventeen, way too old, and also what her parents considered "a loser." Nicki told us how kind and smart and gorgeous he was, and as she talked about him she looked radiant. She had assured her parents that she and Cole were only friends, but they had started sneaking out to be together, and finally they had been caught.

Nicki and Cole had been seen kissing one day after school and all hell had broken loose. Nicki's conservative parents had freaked out. She said her mom actually slapped her when Nicki had tried to explain that Cole was decent and kind, and that he shouldn't be judged for his alcoholic mother or absent father. Her parents forbade her to see him anymore. The next week, Cole and Nicki were spotted by one of Nicki's aunts walking down to the creek, holding hands.

That's when Nicki's dad found a different job so they could move away. Nicki's little brother had been born with some handicaps and Nicki had felt really guilty for stressing her parents even more by carrying on with Cole. She broke it off with him and vowed to move on even though she still loved him. Alameda would be a fresh start for Nicki and her family and she decided not to tell anyone about Cole, to literally forget him. That's why she didn't tell us about him.

I burned a crepe when she said that. I had to look out the window and focus on not yelling at her. She should have told us! I sighed, and Nicki knew what it meant. She gave me a little shrug that said "sorry." What could I say? The girl obviously felt terrible about it all. I slid the burned crepe into the trash and gave her a little grin.

She said she really tried to forget him at first. Our long walks by the bay had helped. But then Cole got her address from the cousin, and started writing to her. When she finally broke down and wrote back, he bought her a cell phone and sent it to her. That's why she had to rush home for a few weeks earlier in the year—she had to get the mail before her parents. I remembered her rushing off, even missing yearbook meetings, for awhile. They started talking every day, mostly late at night, and she knew she still loved him.

M had interrupted her to ask, in a hurt voice, why she didn't tell us at *that* point about Cole. Nicki just shrugged and cried harder. She apologized about twenty times and begged us to forgive her for not trusting us with her secret.

We did, of course. Now Nicki is grounded. Her parents closed down her email account and put her computer in the family room where they can monitor her when she is doing school work. Obviously, the cell phones have been confiscated. They have caller ID and a phone log for incoming calls on their home phone too. Her parents are threatening to send her to some hardcore private school if she has any more contact with Cole. Poor Nicki. She is basically in jail. She is also, obviously, totally in love.

The only reason she got to come over today is because M is leaving for good after this. She says she and

Cole will find a way. We finally finish the crepes, but no one is very hungry anymore.

And then it is time for M to get ready to go to the airport. My dad comes in, and we are all quiet, wordlessly communicating with our eyes. Even though we are about to separate, we are closer than we have ever been.

Crepes of Wrath

3 eggs
1 ¼ C. milk
2 T. vegetable oil
1 C. flour, sifted
½ t. salt
dash cayenne powder
butter

Whisk eggs until frothy, whisk in oil until combined. Mix salt and cayenne into flour. Mix flour into egg mixture, beating until smooth. Put batter into a measuring cup or any container with a spout for easy pouring. Cover with plastic wrap and chill for at least one half hour.

Heat a large, nonstick skillet over medium-high heat. Get batter from fridge, uncover and re-stir. Add one teaspoon butter to hot pan. Butter will melt, then foam, and when the foam subsides your pan is ready. Pick it up and tilt it around so butter covers the bottom. Quickly pour about 2 T. of batter into center of pan, and lift it from burner again, tilting and twirling it quickly so batter covers pan in a circle about the size of a dinner plate. It may take awhile to get the hang of this, but keep trying. Let the crepe cook about one minute, then flip to other side with a rubber spatula and cook one minute on the other side. Slide crepe onto wax paper, layering crepes and wax paper in a stack as you make them. Be sure and add more butter (a teaspoon or so) between each crepe. If the "skin" forms too quickly and thickly, adjust the heat down, if it sticks, use more butter. If they are rubbery and not golden brown after about a minute, turn the heat up. These are tricky to make, but once you get the hang of it they are impressive and can be used for so many things.

Here are some of our favorite ways to eat crepes: Roll them up and sprinkle them with powdered sugar and drizzle with lemon juice; fold up and drizzle with chocolate syrup; spread them with cream cheese and jam, then roll; spread jarred tomato sauce and sprinkle with cheese, add favorite pizza toppings if you want, then roll up and bake for 10 minutes or so at 400°; any fresh fruit makes a good crepe filling, top with whipped cream; layer ham, Swiss cheese, and Dijon mustard, then roll up and bake. Experiment with your own fillings, the possibilities are limitless!

6 Months Later

Epilogue

The small plane's engines rumble loudly as we bank left, making a gradual arc over a stretch of ocean sparkling brightly in the noonday sun. Huge rocks jut out of the water, and as we descend I can see pelicans and seagulls riding invisible cushions of air along the jagged cliffs. Stretching away from the ocean as far as I can see is forest. Deep green and lush, the trees are so dense that I can't see any ground, only their thick foliage. The plane descends sharply now, and for a moment I feel my pulse speed up because it looks like we're going to land in the ocean. Just as suddenly a small landing strip appears surrounded by empty fields.

The airport is a one-building affair here in Crescent City. After the chaos of navigating San Francisco's enormous, crowded airport, this simple place is wonderfully *un*stressful. M and her mom are at the door to greet me as I enter the small building. Their old Volvo is parked just outside, in the nearly-empty parking lot.

As we drive to their new house, M points things out to me along the way. Castle Rock is the rock I saw as we landed. It is home to a huge sea lion colony. Battery Point Lighthouse sits proudly on its own little island, the bright white and red column framed by curving coastline looks like a postcard. It reminds me of some-place on the East Coast somehow. M has her mom drive by the Marine Mammal Rescue Center, where she vol-unteers once a week. She tells me about the baby seals that they nurse to health. We drive by the high school with its bright blue, all-weather track, and M talks about going there next school year.

I listen to her talk. She uses her hands a lot, and talks more quickly than she used to. Her voice is louder, more assured. She looks different too. Her face is lightly tanned, probably from time outside hiking in the red-woods with the hiking group she has joined. Her hair is longer, and there is a blonde, streaky look to it that is quite pretty. She's filled out more too, where she should be, finally. She looks older, but it's more than that. It's more that she has a sort of confidence she never had before. It makes me feel inexplicably sad somehow, that she has come to this place and blossomed, that without me by her side she's moved on so well.

As we drive, M asks about Nicki. Nicki still isn't allowed to have email or a cell phone, and her phone calls at home are monitored by one or the other of her parents. She got caught trying to contact Cole again the first week she got ungrounded. Her parents got even stricter then, and almost made her quit yearbook. She was allowed to go to yearbook meetings only after Ms. Oliver contacted Nicki's parents and pleaded that she be allowed to finish the year. Nicki's parents had agreed only after Ms. Oliver promised to call them immediately if Nicki was ever late or absent. Nicki's yearbook came out last month, and it is a thing of beauty. I have a copy, signed by almost everyone from M's old homeroom, to surprise her with later.

I tell M how I haven't seen Nicki since school got out and yearbook ended. She's practically locked down. We both really miss Nicki, and we worry too. I see my own sadness and fear for Nicki mirrored in M's eyes.

We get to M's house, and she gives me a quick tour. It is bigger and nicer than their old house in Alameda. It sits in a little grove of trees that block out the neighbors. Her room is more spacious too. I flop down on her bed while she answers the ringing phone. It is obviously a friend, and I hear them talking about getting a group together for a beach day. I will be honest, I am jealous.

"Well?" she says after she hangs up.

"What?" I ask.

"What do you think?" She twirls around, her arms

wide. "About all this . . . my house, the town, the beaches."

"It's pretty here, M. Seems perfect." I sound stingy, even to myself. I should be happy for her, but I am not. I expected to come and hear about her boredom and loneliness, how much she missed me. From her emails I thought she might be a little more, I don't know, needful of me, if that makes sense.

"Ariel, it is. Except one thing. The biggest thing."

I wait for her to go on.

"Missing my best friends. Missing you, Air."

And just like that my brain sort of clicks. I have a mental sensation like puzzle pieces are fitting together. It is knowing, I mean *really, really* knowing, that I haven't lost M, but that it will never be the same either. I am relieved but really sad all at once.

"I guess I was worried about that a little," I admit.

"I have made some good friends here, but you can't be replaced, Ariel, ever, you know that. My god, we were potty-trained together. Don't you know that's *deep*?"

I laugh a little. "I guess I wanted things to be exactly the same with us, and they aren't. *You* seem really different."

"But I'm good, *we're* good, you know? It *is* different now. So much has happened. As my mom loves to say, you can't unring a bell."

I nod my head. She's right. Enough heavy stuff

though. "I have something for you." I go to my suitcase and unzip the front compartment.

"A present!" M squeals, grabbing the package and ripping into it. She throws the paper on the ground, and looks at the box.

"I thought it was . . . the perfect thing for you," I tell her.

She laughs. It is a new version of the Game of Life called Game of Life: Twists and Turns. "Yeah, I would say that's about right!"

"We miss you on game nights, M."

She gives the game box a little shake and smiles. "Thanks, Air."

We both sit on her bed, quiet, thinking our own thoughts.

I get up to examine a new pig on her shelf. He is a sailor pig with an eye patch and a life preserver ring slung over his shoulder that says CRESCENT CITY.

"He's a local," M says. I laugh and put him down, then turn back to face her.

"You know, your commercials are still playing on cable back home," I tell M. "You are like a celebrity. It's funny, since you left you got really popular!"

M giggles. "I'll never forget the little people."

"Gee, that's a relief." I shove her arm.

"Wanna go walk the beach trail I was telling you about?"

"Sounds great." And it does. Suddenly I am excited about the adventures in store for us during this week.

"Let's go!"

Her mom drops us off in a parking lot high above the ocean, and gives us strict instructions about what time we need to meet back up to get home. The trailhead looks steep, and I wonder if Endert's Beach is worth what looks to be a challenging hike.

The path is a meandering switchback that gently lowers us down to the ocean. We traverse the narrow trail in silence, our legs brushing wildflowers and ferns. The cliff is so high above the ocean it is scary and thrilling. I make sure to stay well away from the edge.

I suddenly need to ask the universe something. I haven't done it in so long, but in this moment I have to know. Will we be okay? All three of us. *Really* okay? I mutter the question, and ask for a sign. Instantly I regret picking up my old game—if there's no obvious answer, I'll worry.

I try to dismiss it, tell myself the universe game doesn't really work anyway, when we break through the tree line and come onto the sand. It is breathtakingly gorgeous. Craggy shelves of limestone meet a deep blue sea. I hear a distant rumbling that grows into a babble of honking, and a flock of birds flies high above us, forming a perfect double V that looks like a W. There is one individual goose flying way out in front, his neck craned forward. We both stop to watch, hands shielding our eyes, as the birds pass over us. From this perspective the formation makes a perfect M, and I realize the universe has answered.

Recipe Index

Ariel's Measurements and Abbreviations, Cooking Tips, Favorite Tricks, and Generally Useful Things to Know in the Pursuit of Making Fantastic Food

Common abbreviations:

t. or tsp. = teaspoon

T. or TBS. = tablespoon

C. = cup

pinch or dash = 1/8 t.

" = symbol for inch

° = degrees (F = Fahrenheit, C = Celsius)

Terms to Know:

Mix: Nothing fancy, just make sure it's all blended together.

Blend: Pretty much like mixing, but more thoroughly.

Whisk: Use a wire whisk, or a fork if you don't have one, and use a rapid, circular motion to combine ingredients well.

Emulsify: Use a blender or mixer to turn something into liquid.

Zest: Use the finest, tiniest side on your grater to make zest by grating citrus peel.

Brine: Fancy word that just means to soak something in liquid.

Marinate: To put something, usually meat, in a sauce or spice mixture, usually overnight. Oversize ziplocks work great for this.

Coarse or Rough Chopped: Cut up into fairly large chunks; dime-sized or so.

Finely Chopped: Chopped up into small pieces—about the size of an earring back.

Minced: Cut up into super-small pieces—usually have to chop and re-chop whatever you're mincing to get it into really tiny pieces.

Crushed: Usually garlic or herbs are crushed, literally . . . use the handle or the flat side of a large knife to smash the ingredient.

Snipped: Cut up in little pieces with kitchen scissors (or wash regular scissors and use them).

Ground: Powdered. If you have to grind something yourself, a coffee bean grinder works well (wash before and after). Can be done by hand using a mortar/pestle or putting whatever you need to turn into powder into a baggie, covering it with a kitchen towel, and using a mallet or hammer to pulverize.

Interesting Foodie Words

Pith: That white, felt-like stuff between the skin and the fruit on oranges, lemons, and limes. It's bitter and should be picked off or cut off, always.

Seeded: Should really be "unseeded" because this means remove the seeds.

Roux: A French word, pronounced "roo"—it's a mixture
of butter, flour, and milk (sometimes recipes call for
different kinds of fat, and use broth or some other
liquid instead of milk). All chefs know how to make
a basic roux.

Cut "on the bias": Basically, this means to cut something
on a diagonal, making the longest possible slices.

Sifted: Dry ingredients like flour or powdered sugar are
sifted to make sure there are no lumps or "pebbles"—
if you don't have a sifter, put the flour in a strainer
and tap it with you palm over a bowl, or use the back
of a spoon to force it through the mesh.

Slurry: Cornstarch and water mixed together and then
added to something for thickening.

Reduce: Cooking the water out of something until the volume becomes smaller. Like if you needed to reduce a
cup of chicken broth by half, you'd cook it, basically
evaporating the water through steam, until only half
a cup was left.

Stock: Fancy word for a broth or bouillon.

Poaching: Cooking something, usually fish, in a little bit
of stock or other liquid.

Sautéing: Basically frying with a little bit of butter or oil.
Actual "frying" is with a lot of oil or butter, enough to
almost cover what you're cooking, while sautéing is
only enough cooking fat to coat the bottom of the pan.

Blanching: Putting something in boiling water for a
very short time, then removing it and putting it

immediately in ice water. Blanching makes the skin peel off produce and nuts.

Broiling: Cooking something on "broil" (500°) with the oven rack as close to the heat source as possible.

Good, Basic Stuff to Know

— Read through a recipe, including the ingredients and instructions, before starting it. There is nothing worse than being halfway through a recipe and realizing you're out of some key ingredient, or that the dish you planned to serve in an hour is supposed to marinate overnight.

— Always preheat the oven or pan; cakes can fall flat and meats turn tough if they start out "cold cooking."

— Don't ever pour or measure out anything directly over the bowl. I was once pouring a capful of vanilla over my mixing bowl and my fingers slipped and I dropped the whole bottle into the mix. Recipe ruined, and $8.00 bottle of vanilla wasted.

— Measure flour by using a spoon to fill the measuring cup, and then use a butter knife to level it. Don't pack or shake to measure it, or you'll be using too much by accident.

— If a recipe uses eggs, get them out of the fridge at least 15 minutes before using them, and let them "sweat" (you'll see moisture form on the shell as they warm up) so they can come to room temperature.

Especially in baking, room-temperature eggs will be fluffier and rise better. Speaking of eggs, get in the habit of cracking and breaking them in a separate container, not straight into whatever you're making. That way you can see any little shell bits and scrape them out with your fingernail before adding to the recipe.

— Most of the time in baking, you can use margarine and butter interchangeably. Butter makes things (like cookies) more crispy-crumbly, and margarine makes them more soft and chewy. When sautéing or frying, or making sauces, don't substitute margarine for butter because it will burn and separate.

— Speaking of baking, it is very important to follow directions *exactly* when baking breads, cakes, cookies etc. This means measuring everything precisely and not ever skipping steps (like pre-mixing the dry ingredients). Even if a step seems like you could just skip it, DON'T. There are chemical reactions that happen when you are baking, and every step in a recipe is necessary for that to happen right.

— If a recipe calls for a pastry bag, you can use a ziplock baggie. Put the frosting or whatever you are supposed to "pipe" out of a pastry bag and seal. Snip one corner off, and gently squeeze the contents out the hole.

— When using salt and pepper, less is more. Just go easy on both and let people add their own to the finished food. If you do happen to over salt something liquidy (like spaghetti sauce, or a reduction sauce), cut a raw, peeled potato in half and drop it in for a half hour. It'll soak up some of the extra salt (throw it away when you take it out). If you over pepper there's not much to be done.

— Remember that uncooked meat might have bacteria (which are killed when cooked) so wash anything it touches, including the knives and your hands, with hot soap and water. I have one cutting board that I use only for meat, and another that is dedicated to using for chopping up everything else.

— If you are cutting up fresh, hot peppers, wash your hands very thoroughly right after and be sure not to touch your eyes or you'll be "crying" for about a half hour. If onions make you tear-up, put the onion in the freezer for 10 minutes before you cut it. If you have handled garlic or fish and can't get the smell off your cutting board or your skin, rub half a lemon over the smelly areas.

— When cooking meats, they need to "rest" (come out of the oven or pan and sit) for at least a few minutes before eating them. The natural juices need to settle and redistribute, and the meat actually keeps cooking internally for a few minutes after it comes off the heat (I always find this weird). If the recipe says to "tent" the resting meat, use a piece of foil to just loosely cover it like a tent (don't pull it tight or tuck it in).

— My most important tip about cooking involves something I struggle with all the time—failure. I have been crushed when a recipe I slaved over made my family practically gag, or bread I made exactly as described in the recipe came out of the oven flat and hard, or some recipe that everyone raved about online is barely mediocre. The thing to remember is that it is going to happen—maybe you missed a step by accident, maybe an ingredient was bad and you didn't know . . . and people's tastes are so personal and different it's just hard to make stuff everyone likes all the time. It's impossible actually. I don't let it get me down anymore, because if I did I couldn't keep on this chef path.

Essential Tools for the Kitchen

It is really easy to get this stuff, even on a budget. Check out dollar stores, thrift shops, garage sales, and even antique stores for cool, sometimes even vintage, cooking stuff. Places like Target, Rite Aid, and even the grocery stores sell cooking tools, dishes, and small appliances, sometimes very cheaply. You just have to stay on the look out and build your kitchen supplies slowly and steadily.

Must Have

— A full body apron
— Several measuring cups, in different sizes (I like the plastic nesting ones that go in the dishwasher)

- 1 large (4 cup or more) Pyrex measuring cup (that's a kind of glass that can be microwaved, put in the oven, etc.—very tough)
- A complete set of teaspoon and tablespoon measuring spoons
- A good, sturdy cutting board, preferably two (one dedicated to meat)
- Several wooden spoons
- A set of different-sized mixing bowls
- A handheld, electric mixer
- A box grater (has different types of grating on each side to handle everything from cheese to zest)
- A potato peeler
- A wire whisk, pair of tongs, spatula, rubber scraper, meat mallet, ladle, slotted spoon
- A couple of good, sharp knives
- A colander, to use for draining pasta, rinsing produce, sifting flour, etc.
- A set of cookie sheets (don't confuse with a jelly roll pan, which has a "lip" all the way around the edges; Cookie sheets are flat, without edges on the long sides)
- A jelly roll pan
- A set of pots and frying pans, various sizes
- Several baking dishes, various sizes

Not Vital, But Makes Life in the Kitchen Much Better

- KitchenAid countertop mixer
- Blender

- Salad spinner
- Immersion handheld blender (Fits in the hand, and can be put into liquids and hot stuff as it cooks, to blend. Also makes individual fruit smoothies in the cup.)
- Rice cooker
- Crock pot
- Mini kitchen scale (some European and ethnic recipes give amounts in weights)
- Meat thermometer
- Mandolin slicer (This is a slicer that is a platform with a really sharp blade mounted in it, and you slice the food—like potatoes or cucumbers—by passing it over the mounted blade. Use the hand guard, as one slice on your thumb can be super-serious. The blade is so sharp and it is angled to really cut. This is the best way to slice things paper-thin and evenly.)

Places I Go For Help, Recipes, or Definitions

- I love magazine recipes. I get *Cooking Light* and *Cook's Illustrated,* and my mom gets a bunch of mom magazines like *Family Circle* and *Oprah* that have recipes too. Our library sells old issues of all sorts of magazines for a quarter each, so I get stacks of those to go through too. I use a three-ring binder to keep good recipes I rip out. Each time I try out a recipe, I make notes about it—like that it needs more salt, or that the cooking time should be longer.

- Secondhand, consignment, and thrift stores always have fantastic selections of old and newer cookbooks.
- Send away for free cookbooks offered as promotional and advertising material by some companies or brands. For example, the Philadelphia Cream Cheese Brand Cookbook is phenomenal. The company wants you to love, buy, and cook with their product, so they work hard to put out really good, well-tested recipes. The same is true for the recipes printed on packaging. For example, my favorite couscous recipe is a version of one I tried off the side of the Near East couscous box.
- There are tons of online sources for recipes. Be sure to read user ratings and comments—I have found I get the best idea about a recipe by reading about the experience other cooks had making and eating the recipe. If you are going to attempt a new technique, like making a roux, try an online tutorial course first for free from about.com or cooks.com. Wikipedia.org is a great source to use for definitions of cooking terms.
- Cooking shows are a fantastic way to learn because you can actually *see* the chefs making stuff and imitate their techniques. They also have a lot of great recipes. Rachael Ray is the best, in my never humble opinion, at showing how to cook good, simple food. The Food Network is a cable channel that is all

cooking all the time and has a great variety of stuff
to watch and try.

— If you are eating out and love a dish, you can ask
the waiter if it would be possible to get the recipe.
Sometimes they can't, or won't, but sometimes, especially in smaller, non-chain restaurants, they will
give it to you.

My Top Cookbooks of All Time

Joy of Cooking, by Irma S. Rombauer and Marion
Rombauer Becker. Considered the Bible of cooking.

The Classic Italian Cookbook, by Marcella Hazan. The
best *ever* Italian cookbook.

The Gourmet Cookbook, by Ruth Reichl. It has *everything!*

Sixty-Minute Gourmet, by Pierre Franey. Impressive
meals you really can make in an hour.

In 2009, thanks to the Milkweed Prize for Children's Literature, I was invited into middle schools throughout the Midwest and California to speak with students. I met a generation of young people who are creative, hopeful, and courageous. They reminded me how hard it is to be stuck somewhere between childhood and adulthood, and how important it is to tell stories about being wedged in that small space. Thank you to all the kids who shared their own stories about being there. This book is for you.

Julie Crabtree won the Milkweed Prize for Children's Literature for her novel *Discovering Pig Magic*. She has also been published in the *San Francisco Chronicle Magazine, Highlights for Children, MotherVerse, Green Prints,* and *Knowledge Quest.* She received her BA from the University of California at Davis in English and her paralegal certificate. Julie worked as a legal administrator until 1999, when she became a freelance writer. She lives with her family in the Pacific Northwest.

If you enjoyed this book, you'll also want to read these other Milkweed novels.

To order books or for more information, contact Milkweed at (800) 520-6455
or visit our Web site (www.milkweed.org).

Discovering Pig Magic
Julie Crabtree

Perfect
Natasha Friend

The Keening
A. LaFaye

Slant
Laura E. Williams

Milkweed Editions

Founded in 1979, Milkweed Editions is one of the largest independent, nonprofit literary publishers in the United States. Milkweed publishes with the intention of making a humane impact on society, in the belief that good writing can transform the human heart and spirit.

Join Us

Milkweed depends on the generosity of foundations and individuals like you, in addition to the sales of its books. In an increasingly consolidated and bottom-line-driven publishing world, your support allows us to select and publish books on the basis of their literary quality and the depth of their message. Please visit our Web site (www.milkweed.org) or contact us at (800) 520-6455 to learn more about our donor program.

Milkweed Editions, a nonprofit publisher, gratefully acknowledges sustaining support from Amazon.com; Emilie and Henry Buchwald; the Bush Foundation; the Patrick and Aimee Butler Foundation; Timothy and Tara Clark; the Dougherty Family Foundation; Friesens; the General Mills Foundation; John and Joanne Gordon; Ellen Grace; William and Jeanne Grandy; the Jerome Foundation; the Lerner Foundation; Sanders and Tasha Marvin; the McKnight Foundation; Mid-Continent Engineering; the Minnesota State Arts Board, through an appropriation by the Minnesota State Legislature and a grant from the National Endowment for the Arts; Kelly Morrison and John Willoughby; the National Endowment for the Arts; the Navarre Corporation; Ann and Doug Ness; Jörg and Angie Pierach; the Carl and Eloise Pohlad Family Foundation; the RBC Foundation USA; the Target Foundation; the Travelers Foundation; Moira and John Turner; and Edward and Jenny Wahl.

Interior design by Ann Sudmeier
Typeset in Warnock Pro
by BookMobile Design and Publishing Services
Printed on acid-free 45# Alternative Book Cream paper
by Friesens Corporation